I0567252

LOVE,
MY NEIGHBOR

A novel of faith

BRENT MONAHAN

Also by Brent Monahan

DeathBite (with Michael Maryk)
Satan's Serenade
The Uprising
The Book of Common Dread
The Blood of the Covenant
The Bell Witch - An American Haunting
The Jekyl Island Club
The Sceptred Isle Club
The Manhattan Isle Club
Nevermore - A Novel of Edgar Allan Poe and Allan Pinkerton
Time Step

All of the events, characters, names and places depicted herein are fictional or used fictitiously. No representation is made that any of the statements made in this novel are true or that any incident depicted in this novel actually occurred, nor is any of the same intended or should be inferred by the reader.

Love, My Neighbor - A Novel of Faith
Copyright © 2013 by Brent Monahan

All rights reserved. No part of this book may be reproduced, transmitted or stored whole, in part or in any manner whatsoever without the written permission, except in the case of brief quotations embodied in critical articles or reviews. For information, please contact Words Take Flight Books (http://www.wtfbooks.net).

ISBN 13: 978-0615822921
ISBN 10: 0615822924

Printed in the United States of America

*Dedicated to Pastor Michael A. McKillip
on the occasion of his installation
at St. John Evangelical Lutheran Church,
Yardley, Pennsylvania*

CHAPTER ONE

THERE ARE PEOPLE, even in our little town of Bunhouse, New Jersey, who believe that the story of Ernest Love is purely about outdoor illumination. As one who lives on Ernie's street, I can tell you firsthand that those folk don't know the heart of the story. Garish Christmas decorations merely shed light on the darkness reclaiming our egocentric world and the crying need for rebirth.

If you're ever in the market for dead deer, Ernest Love proved that they're not hard to get. Soon after Thanksgiving, he drove to the local yard where agents of the Animal Control Commission drop off the road kill they collect. He claimed to be an amateur tanner newly moved to the area, looking for hides to cure and meat to freeze for his hunting dogs. He purchased nine of the least-injured carcasses and loaded them into a rented U-Haul.

Bunhouse is one of the well-heeled bedroom communities that feed New York and Philadelphia with harried professionals like my husband. They commute too many hours each day to be able to say they live where life is more relaxed. The houses have three rooms serving the same function as did their parents' one living room. The cathedral ceilings hold more useless hot air than a presidential convention. They're stuffed with furniture people rarely sit on and toys, fads and techno-gimmicks that Madison Avenue tells us we can't enjoy life without. To pay for all this upscale clutter we work four more weeks a year than the Germans and five more than the Italians. There's enough room in between our houses that we can barely hear each other hollering at our spoiled kids. The downside is meadow-sized lawns we need to pay a service to cut. The plumber, electrician, duct cleaner, carpet cleaner and chimney cleaner all take one look at these piles of brick and stone and tack an extra twenty percent onto our bills because "they can afford it" – which is possibly the greatest irony of our lives.

Ernest Love lived in our community, but he was not a part of it. He was not what the boys at the bottom of the block called "a team player." That fact had been confirmed months earlier, but the extent of its truth did not become clear until after the early December snowstorm.

Until that day, at least to the casual viewers, on Skytop Road all was calm – even if all were not bright. As the last snowflakes settled to earth from vanishing lead-colored clouds, the nine dead deer appeared on Neighbor Love's front lawn, linked together by what looked to be a harness. A vintage airplane propeller rose like a cemetery monument among their mangled carcasses. Clement Moore had collided with Charles Lindbergh. Dancer lay on his back with all four legs pointing straight up. Cupid planted a frozen kiss on Vixen's butt. A pair of glittering red stars covered Comet's eyes. A gleaming, candy-apple-colored sleigh hung upside down from one of the two, bare-branched maple trees directly behind the manufactured "reindeer," defying gravity on near-invisible piano wire. Out of a snow bank poked a pair of black boots and the bottoms of red flannel pants. Several stuffed canvas bags were strewn across the snow, and a few gaily-wrapped packages spilled from their open mouths. The window decorators at Macy's Herald Square could not have produced a more arresting tableau. Strung between the trees and above the wreckage, a long plastic banner proclaimed in two-foot-high red letters: **Xmas Canceled This Year**. As neighbor Joe Ciaro later remarked, "It didn't even say 'Christmas,' ferchrissake!"

Ernie Love had put a great deal of thought and effort into his creation. The sleigh-guiding reindeer did not merely sport a blinking light on the end of his snout; the brilliant little halogen bulb was hidden under a red plastic clown nose bought at The Party Store. Ernie had skillfully fed the wires from the bulb into Rudolph's nostrils, so that the batteries were completely hidden. Each "reindeer" had antlers, fashioned from tree branches and secured to its skull via bored holes and liberal applications of Gorilla Glue. Most amazingly, the provocative scene had appeared as if literally fallen from the sky. Before the storm, not one holiday bulb decorated Love's front lawn. By the time the whiteout had faltered to well-spaced flakes, there was the triple-spotlighted extravaganza, glowing in glory. I pulled on my husband's Mighty Mac, stabbed my feet into his unlaced Frye boots, and trudged outside to measure its impact from the deserted street. The harness bells, jingling softly in the wind, afforded a particularly poignant touch.

According to Ernie Love, he had started nothing but had rather reacted to the pressure of Skytop Road's Illumination Mafia. The mob's self-proclaimed don and enforcer was one Hubert Jasse, known as Hugh. He resided with his long-suffering family at the bottom of the hill and engineered winter displays that were featured year after year in local newspapers and on television news broadcasts. His 1998 "Salute to Universal Peace" had earned him a photo and two paragraphs on a break page of the Sunday *Times of Trenton*. That triumph had assured him that his displays were a matter of manifest destiny. The year of the reindeer incident, he incorporated no fewer than eighteen thousand lights and six animated stations, along with an electronic Times Square ticker that constantly cycled out the message "Santa Goes High Tech for Christmas." Animated elves worked with Craftsman radial saws, Black and Decker motorized screwdrivers, and Stanley drills above a conveyor belt of endlessly streaming toys. Into the street drifted the sounds of "Santa Baby," again and again and again.

Harry Covair and Joe Ciaro, Hugh's henchmen who lived on either side, only added incrementally to their extravaganzas from year to year, but these burned no fewer kilowatts. Together, the three houses rivaled the Las Vegas Strip. But this was not enough for the trio. Through encouragement, intimidation and even outright bribery, they had convinced every other family on the street to present elaborate holiday displays. Even the Rothmans attached a ten-foot-high menorah to their chimney and offered a large, blue, illuminated, revolving dreidel on their lawn. We were lucky enough to have planted a blue spruce in our front yard when we moved in. Our five-hundred, well-strung white twinkle lights, along with the high-impact plastic miniature deer and the imitation bunny-fur snowshoe rabbits staring in wonder at their glow, were enough to pacify the pageant-pushing posse.

But Peace on Earth was not to be perpetual.

Ernest Love had, in fact, moved onto Skytop Road in mid-November of the previous year, during the season that Hugh had unveiled his "Tribute to Christmas in Russia," a late celebration of the reemergence of Christianity following the collapse of Soviet communism. The Hermitage, with St. Nick's red-white-and-blue miniature sleigh on its roof, might not have touched off the powder keg, but a babushka-ed Babafana dancing beside Lenin's Kremlin tomb struck the necessary spark. Three days after moving in, Ernie

Love dared the pitch of his icy garage roof to staple the message "Xmas…Bolshoi," spelled out with six strings of randomly arranged orange-and-pink lights that pulsed on and off like a lighthouse beacon. The message was tantamount to waving Santa's coat in front of three bulls: it only spurred Hugh, Harry and Joe to greater efforts the next year.

The Illumination Mafia annually took their cue from the Quakerbridge Mall as to the socially acceptable date for unveiling holiday displays. Unfortunately, the mall bigwigs had fired their display coordinator in June and, in so doing, pushed the divine birthday event all the way back to October 1st. October 2nd that year was a miserable day, but if "…neither snow nor sleet nor gloom nor dark of night…" could stay mere postal couriers from their appointed rounds, no freezing rain could deter the High-tension Trio. In the course of twelve frenzied hours, numbers 1, 3 and 5 Skytop Road went from mere domiciles to runway 57 at O'Hare. Holiday bonuses were guaranteed for everyone in the Public Service Electric and Gas Company.

Having lived on stately Skytop Road for twenty-two years, I know the names of all the adults on the block, what they do for a living, and what they drive. Naturally, I have a better rapport with the people in the houses nearest me. I know their favorite vacation spots, their political proclivities, and what the insides of their homes look like. I could not say the same about next-door neighbor Ernest Love after thirteen months. The day he arrived, he had the Mayflower truck backed up almost to the garage doorframe, just as he did with the U-Haul the next year when he sneaked in the dead deer. Mrs. Dorothea Riley across the street, she of the twenty-power tripod-mounted binoculars, was livid with frustration.

To say that our newest neighbor kept to himself was an understatement. He did not speak unless spoken to. In spite of housewarming gifts of baked bread and cookies and a spate of verbal ice-breaking stratagems among the "high number" Skytop contingent, the solitary inhabitant never invited anyone inside his house. We all knew its layout from the fact that a third of the homes on the road were built in that configuration. But of his belongings we were as ignorant as the average American voter is of the contents of the Bill of Rights.

It was not that Ernie was rude. He invariably replied to a hello. He was pleasant and almost garrulous once you got him started, so long as you stuck to non-personal topics like the weather, the New York and Philadelphia professional sports teams, or when to get a flu shot.

Regarding his contribution to the property value of the neighborhood, he more than did his part. His predecessors, divorcee Fifi Rogers and her teenage sons, had not been instinctive homeowners. To them, taking care of property meant mowing the weeds just before the mailbox disappeared and not leaving the emptied garbage cans on the street for more than three days. Under the Rogers family's assiduous neglect, what was once a handsome house had deteriorated to something from a Charles Addams cartoon. Within eight months of moving in, Ernie had replaced the roof shingles, painted the house a "tea with cream" tan, repaired the chimney, reseeded the lawn, trimmed back the hedges, replaced the Kresges curtains with stylish Levelors, and planted beds of geraniums and Sweet Williams. But nobody knew his politics, his religion, or his taste in interior decor. Nobody knew where he vacationed or if he vacationed. And nobody could fathom why this single man who looked to be in his early forties lived alone in a Colonial house with four bedrooms and two-and-a-half baths.

I live with my husband, William, and my son, Liam, in the same style house that Ernie owns. Our lives, however, are open books. We also have a daughter, Gabrielle, at Yale, pursuing a degree in drama while our plans for retirement recede into the next millennium. Liam attends high school, Will sells equipment to fire companies, and I work from home as a free-lance journalist.

In spring, summer, and fall, while waiting for flashes of inspiration, I often garden. It was during such outdoor hours that I communed with Ernest Love. In truth, whenever I spotted him working on his yard, I found an excuse to wander to that side of my property line and make neighborly noises. By the end of his first summer on Skytop Road, he knew a great deal about me and my family. But I knew almost nothing of him. His penchant for privacy seemed pathological. When I got up the courage to ask point blank, "Where did you come from before moving here?" he answered, "Oh, lots of places." I confided his fiercely private nature to the "high number" Skytop neighbors, and this, of course, fueled wild speculations. Every now and then, he went away on short trips. Early on, I volunteered to collect his mail for him while he was away, but he told me that he had rented a large mail slot down at the Bunhouse post office. He was the proverbial enigma wrapped in a riddle cocooned inside a conundrum, and the neighborhood did not take kindly to his minding his own business. He did not respond to Dorothea's mailing on behalf of the March of Dimes. He did not participate in the Neighborhood Watch. His lights were not on for Halloween.

Voltaire wrote that "If God did not exist, we would have to invent Him." Similarly, if a neighbor does not exist whom we can disapprove of and suspect, we will appoint and then create one. Speculations about Ernest Love served to fill especially dull dinnertime conversations up and down Skytop Road. But the reindeer display was like a stout chew bone that every cur could sink his canines into whenever he was bored.

Hardly had the last snowflake of the storm tumbled from the sky when Hugh and his henchmen were at the edge of Love's property, peering and pacing, daring three feet beyond the curb to snap close-ups of the furry corpses. Hugh had his Olympus digital camera flashing while Virgil panned the scene with his Sony Camcorder. Joe took a couple shots with his cell phone. When they at last retreated in a pack, I am certain they made even better use of their communications equipment.

What made Ernest Love's display doubly vexing to the trio was the obvious decrease in outdoor decoration tonnage among the "high number" Skytop homes compared with the previous year. As Hugh captured his images, he was overheard to say that Love's Xmas…Bolshoi had clearly cowed our half of the street into toning down our God-given right to electrified holiday merriment. I believe the tone-down had very little to do with Ernie Love's rooftop message. The truth was that dozens of ropes of made-in-China lights had either balled up hopelessly in basement boxes or else had one impossibly undetectable bulb per parallel strand burn out. Neighbors had simply gotten tired of replacing an overabundance of lights, swearing at icicle configurations that would not unkink, and enduring hours on metal ladders in sub-freezing temperatures they could otherwise have misspent eating cookies and watching football games.

Around ten o'clock the next morning, the vehicular parade began in earnest. Skytop Road is not a main thoroughfare. Most of the year if ten cars an hour pass by, it signifies a party at somebody's house. From early November until Epiphany, however, the accrued fame of our collective holiday displays causes mildly irritating traffic. On this momentous day, the bumper-to-bumper crush resembled Mecca at Ramadan.

The police cruiser did not arrive until noon, inching up the hill behind a vintage Volkswagen Beetle so packed with teenagers that it looked like a circus clown car. I was shoveling out the walkway that my husband and son had both conveniently overlooked. The patrolman pulled into Love's driveway, took his time sauntering to the front door, and knocked, first with gloved hand and then with his nightstick. When no one answered, he stalked away, shaking his head, and muttering with enough force that his words became visible in the frigid air.

That evening, while I was emptying our mailbox of Christmas cards, bills, and the six-hundredth catalogue of the season, Ernie pulled onto his ice-dappled drive. He emerged from his Volvo wearing a well-padded parka and a U.S. Army tundra cap with the ear flaps standing out like Dumbo on the diving platform. His wire-rimmed glasses fogged swiftly with the change of climate from auto to outdoors.

"A policeman was here around noon," I called out to him.

"I figured." He did not look at all fazed. "I checked my answering machine this afternoon. There was a message from the chief of police."

"What did he say?" I asked, expecting the usual oblique non-response.

"I'm not allowed to display dead animals on my property. But he didn't recite any specific law."

"I'm sure the boys at the bottom of the street complained," I ventured.

He wrestled his empty garbage can out of a snowdrift. "It could have been anyone." As if to make his point, he paused and waved merrily at the slightly-parted curtain in Dorothea Riley's window. "That doesn't matter. I would have been disappointed if it didn't stir up a tempest." He didn't bother to mention the teapot.

I confided that I harbored little affection for the trio. When he failed to thank me for my support, I added, "So, when will you get rid of the deer?"

"When they tell me point blank that I have to," he replied. "You and Will ready for the holidays?"

I told him I guessed we were. This was the longest

conversation I had had with Ernie Love since leaf raking, and despite the cold I determined to keep it going. "I mean, I've done all my shopping. Wrote out my cards and mailed 'em yesterday. Our church choir has Bach's *Christmas Cantata* ready to go. And I've got my part memorized for our Living Nativity. I'm the grumpy innkeeper's wife."

Love nodded slowly several times as I spoke, in a manner that usually indicates the hearer wants you to think he's listening.

"You're a member of St. Mark's Church down on the corner of Main and Millpond, aren't you?"

"That's right. Why don't you stop by the Nativity? It's on the grounds; you don't even need to come inside," I invited. Our Living Nativity is one of the church's major annual events. A columnist in the local newspaper once called it "the county's most inspiring Christmas presentation," which made the entire congregation proud as Yuletide punch.

"When is it?"

I told him. He shook his head, as I knew he would.

"Busy that weekend."

A Humvee rolled slowly by Love's tableau mordant. The machine was easy to identify; few people have their Humvees custom-painted pink. The driver was Gladys Crescendo, the wife of the town baker. Her passenger was Francine Higgenbotham, of Higgenbotham Jewelers. Both women were swaddled in dead animal skins. Gladys rolled down her window and thrust out her left hand, middle finger upraised. "You atheists got no respect for the Lord!" she shouted. Francine decided to flip her cigarette at Ernie through Gladys's window, but Gladys had already pressed the power control. The butt struck the rising glass with a shower of red sparks, rebounded smartly, and came to rest, filter-end down, within the collar hairs of Glady's Blackglama mink. Both women screamed. The window lowered again. I stooped and scooped up a ball of snow. Dredging up my old high school pitching skills, I winged the snowball directly at the smoldering butt. What did not extinguish the fire knocked the diamond-encrusted bauble from Gladys's ear.

"Christ Almighty, ya dumb bitch!" she thanked me.

Love absorbed the entire incident with no reaction. He started up his driveway and called over his shoulder, "If I don't see you again before then, Anna, have a good holiday."

I wished him the same. I could have sworn his last words sounded like "holy day."

That was December 18th.

The Animal Control Commission removed the deer on December 20th, leaving behind the bottom half of Santa, the sleigh, the sign and the presents

The *Bunhouse Beacon* arrives in mailboxes on Thursdays. Two days before Christmas, page three was filled with Skytop Road who-what-where-and-when (but no 'why,' since Ernie Love refused to be interviewed) along with photographs of **Xmas Canceled This Year**. An op-ed column on page thirteen, written by the editor with the usual care, contained one spelling, two syntactical and three grammatical errors. The column closed with the unassailable wisdom: "Enough discord darkens the world at this darkest time of the year without crackpot Scrooges adding fuel to the fire."

On Christmas Eve, a present sailed through a pane of Ernest Love's bay window. The rock was worthless, but everyone knows that on Christmas it's the thought that counts. I assumed it was someone without sin getting even on Jesus' behalf.

CHAPTER TWO

I AM RARELY in my backyard in January, so my fence rail communication system with Ernie Love was on seasonal suspension. I do not think he would have mentioned a court summons at any rate. Somebody in the municipal building, however, must have blabbed to the press, because a week before the scheduled hearing, a little article appeared in the *Bunhouse Beacon*. All it said was that Ernest Love, residing at 18 Skytop Road, had received a summons for the following Thursday afternoon, to appear before Judge Dominick Cassato.

Now, I do not consider myself an old fishwife, nosey Norbert, or…if one is classically educated…a *quid nunc*. I don't seek out all my town's gossip or make sure I know who is doing what to whom or who feels this way about that and the other. Somehow, I just happened to know that Dominick Cassato could not have been more Roman Catholic if he was the pope. His father had been a grand poohbah in the Knights of Columbus, his mother had been in charge of the altar guild at St. Jude since the Beatles had long hair, his sister was a nun with the Sisters of Perpetual Grief, and he had made a pilgrimage to Rome and attended a Mass celebrated by the pontiff himself at St. Peter's. I would have believed it looked like somebody had stacked the deck against Ernie, except that Nick Cassato judged all the local civil cases.

One of the perks of working from home is making your own schedule. There was no way I was going to miss this hearing. Some fifty other people had the same idea, so that Bunhouse's little courtroom was packed. The municipality had its prosecutor, Athol Cramp, ready to earn a tiny fraction of the bloated retainer he was annually paid, but Ernie Love sat alone at the defendant's table. The room buzzed until the bailiff announced Dominick Cassato's entrance, and then suddenly you could have heard the pin drop from a hand grenade.

"I must admit that the matter brought before me today," Cassato began after the reading of the complaint, "is unusual. Because of this I would like to see if we can proceed in an informal manner. Dr. Love."

The unexpected title produced a brief wave of subdued noise. I found myself wishing I knew what the judge knew.

Ernie stood. "Yes, your Honor."

"I'd like to give you the opportunity to explain yourself regarding the display on your front lawn during a portion of the month of December just past."

"It was the exercise of free speech, pure and simple, Your Honor," Ernie said in a calm, clear voice. "Since the Bill of Rights appended to United States Constitution protects me in this regard, I respectfully ask that the complaint be dropped."

The Prosecutor Cramp rose to speak, but Magistrate Cassato held up his hand and kept his eyes on my next-door neighbor. "Regarding your display as free speech is, I must say, a rather liberal interpretation. Was the intent of your display humorous or provocative?"

"The display was what it was. I have nothing to add."

The judge glanced briefly at Hugh Jasse, Harry Covair and Joe Ciaro, who sat like "See, Speak and Hear No Evil" in the back row. He turned his head once more toward Ernie, lowered his chin and regarded him through his hawkish eyebrows. "The issue of free speech did not allow you to lie to the Animal Control officer when he asked you the purpose of purchasing nine dead deer. Furthermore, you neglected…or perhaps willfully refused…to respond to an order from this court to dispose of these same animals, so that Animal Control was obliged to remove them for you. Am I accurate?"

The prosecutor harrumphed dramatically at having his thunder stolen. He blew his nose loudly into a monogrammed handkerchief so that nobody could forget he was in the courtroom.

"I was waiting for the day after Christmas, sir. At that point—"

"—you thought," said the judge, completing the thought, "you had a right to stretch the specific order of the court?"

"Your Honor—"

"Yes or no?"

"I am attempting to provide the context that will explain my 'yes or no'."

Cassato rocked back in his chair. "Be brief."

"Have you driven or walked on Skytop Road between early October and early January, Your Honor?"

"I have not."

Ernest opened a large envelope he had set on the defendant's table. He turned it down and shook it. Several photographs tumbled out. "May I approach the bench?"

The judge crooked his fingers. The defendant brought the photos forward. Cassato accepted them and took his time studying each. After a minute, he handed the collection back.

"My display is no more excessive and certainly no more sacrilegious than these," Ernie argued.

"What do you mean sacrilegious?" Jasse cried out, leaping to his feet, making the courtroom further reverberate with the noise of sliding chair legs.

"It means 'against religion,' even though it sounds like the opposite," Harry told him as he coaxed him back onto his chair, in a voice meant to be intimate but more than loud enough for half the courtroom to hear.

Hugh swung his wrath-reddened face at his henchman. "Shut up, Harry! I know what it means." Jasse raised his hands in supplication toward the judge. "Does he have a photo of his last year's display: 'Xmas...Bolshoi'?"

Cassato's gavel came down hard. "The informality of these proceedings does not extend to observers. There will be no more outbursts. And, for your information, Mr. Jasse, 'bolshoi' means 'big' in Russian."

The trio shuffled, scratched, and studied their fingernails.

Judge Cassato looked again at the defendant. "The essential difference is that the displays in these photos do not involve dead animals. I believe I understand your position, Dr. Love. However, the profligate use of kilowatt hours has not been determined to be a health hazard to our community. Nor can matters of taste be successfully argued. In consideration of your spotless record to this date and your level of education, I see no point in having you serve time or pay a fine."

"What the—"

Joe Ciaro was a man of few words, and most of those the four letter variety. Anticipating his neighbor's reaction, Harry clapped his thin right hand over Joe's mouth just in time.

The judge leaned more closely to his microphone. "However,

Dr. Love, the law was ignored, and some penalty must be paid. I find you guilty of nonfeasance in the compliance of a court order and require you to spend fifty hours in community service. Are you a member of a specific religious faith?"

"I was at one time, but no longer."

"A Christian faith?"

"Protestant."

Cassato looked slightly pained at this news. "Since your display was directed, at least tangentially, at the Christian faith, and since it managed to offend a portion of its believers, I suggest that you do your service in one of this community's Protestant houses of worship. The choice is yours."

Ernie sucked in his cheeks. He looked directly at me. "St. Mark's."

Judge Cassato nodded soberly. "This matter is concluded." His gavel came down again. In spite of what Dominick Cassato had pronounced, I had the distinct feeling the matter had just begun.

Directly after the hearing, Ernie approached me and asked what my church might need in the way of service

"You're handy," I said, thinking of the re-shingling he had done on his own home, the exterior walls he had painted and all the intricate wiring done on the deer.

"I suppose."

"We had to let our custodian go."

"Budget problems?" he asked.

A little belly laugh escaped me. "Oh, we always have budget problems. But the custodian used to be a congregant named Darryl Rumplemeyer. We got less for what we spent on him than lottery players do on their tickets. Before he retired, he worked in a junkyard. That's about how he kept the church. If cleanliness is next to godliness, our church was sliding steadily toward Hell. When we let him go, he quit the church."

"Naturally," Ernie said.

I did not ask why his reply had such conviction. It seemed to me ironic, considering he had admitted in court that he had given up his own faith. I said, "Now, a few of the older ladies do the light housekeeping. But we need the tile floors stripped and re-waxed, some bad wiring replaced, a bit of roof patching. And we're always having trouble with the boiler and the air conditioning. A guy named

Burt is in charge of the Maintenance Committee. I'll send you his number," I said in a breezy tone. "You must have an e-mail address."

"Just write it on a piece of paper and slip it behind my storm door," said the Grand Keeper of Secrets.

CHAPTER THREE

I HAD JUST finished editing a piece on "The Best Household Cleaning Tips" for *Good Housekeeping* when my doorbell rang. Ralph the Wonder Mutt – our combination Cocker, Springer and Surprise Spaniel – skittered toward the door and let out the same series of barks he does when the cookie timer goes off. He continued to growl even after I opened to Dorothea Riley. She smiled so broadly at the dog I thought her false teeth would fall out.

"Goodness! Don't you know me after all these years?" she asked, omitting Ralph's name because she doesn't know him after all these years.

To his credit, Ralph dislikes Dorothea. I sent him slinking to the laundry room with a few crisp words and invited my neighbor from across the street as far in as the entry. Dorothea had been a widow for five years. Her husband had died in self-defense.

Dorothea checked what she could of the living and dining rooms, to see if anything had changed. As her eyes wandered, she asked, "You know Renee down on Coventry Lane, don't you?"

"Only to nod at," I answered.

"Well, don't expect her to nod back soon. Something might break. She must have tired of the Botox shots, because she went for a face lift." Dorothea's eyes rolled dramatically. She subscribed to the maxim, 'If you don't have anything mean to say, don't say anything at all.' "She looks like a Jack o' lantern! I hope for her sake her skin relaxes soon. Talk about vanity. Couldn't she have at least waited until she was fifty five?"

"How old is she?"

"I have no idea. Listen, what about Ernie Love? Have you been following up on the news that he's a doctor?"

I told her I had not.

"I figured since you write those magazines articles, you'd be naturally curious and could find out in a flash."

"Dr. Love's private life is no business of mine," I said, telling the truth in the legal, if not the private, sense.

"That's what Joan and Joyce Anne said also," Dorothea sniffed, "but I don't believe them." She paused. "Well," she continued when I failed to fall to the floor from her indirect attack. "I investigated all of Middlesex, Mercer, Hunterdon and Burlington Counties. Used the phone books and all the online HMO directories. He's not listed."

"Some doctors have private numbers," I suggested. "Ironically, my gynecologist does."

Dorothea shrugged as if in acceptance but plowed on. "Do you have any suggestions where I might look next?"

Rather than tell her what I was thinking, I said, "Pennsylvania is just across the river. Have you tried the Bucks, Montgomery and Philadelphia County phone books?"

Dorothea blinked her myopic eyes through her thick spectacles. "No. Good idea." She sniffed the air in vain for molecules of baked goods she might invite herself to. "Well…I'll let you know if I find something out."

I thanked her and swung the door back in a clear invitation for her to skedaddle. She departed on foot power, having left her broom at home.

Having betrayed Mrs. Riley's nosey nature here in print, I cannot take the high road and deny that I had never tried to learn more about Ernest Love. One morning, shortly after the court appearance, I happened to be driving to an early appointment with the aforementioned Ob/Gyn at Princeton Medical Center when I found myself in the daily southbound U.S. Route 1 traffic jam only one car behind Ernie's dark purple Volvo. He and I went through the Princeton traffic circle and both turned west on Alexander Road. I lost him when I got stuck at the light on Faculty Road. Two mornings after that, I lay in wait for him in a parking lot on the other side of that traffic light. I followed him all the way up to Princeton Pike, where he turned left. At that point, I abandoned my surveillance. As far as I was concerned, I had solved the mystery.

Dr. Love had turned into the heart of the Princeton Theological Seminary. What could a minister no longer allowed to have a pastorate or to administer sacraments do with all his theological knowledge? "Those who can't, teach," right? In fact, in these modern times, with dogma flying out the stained-glass windows, such institutions seem to be filling up with people who concentrate more on the history of theology, on comparative literatures of world religions, on making Jesus more of a man and less of a god and explaining away such things as miracles and the power of prayer. Building such curriculums and inviting such faculty make no sense to me, but I do know that if I was the Loyal Opposition, the place where I'd most want to work my dark ways would be where God's mortal colonels and generals are being trained.

Have you ever been in a situation where finding an answer only created a new set of questions? As I turned back for home, more than a little disappointed with myself for spying on Dr. Love, my head ached with questions.

On the second Sunday after his court date, Ernie Love appeared in our church. He arrived at 8:15, with just enough time for me to introduce him to Burt, the property committee chairman, before the first service. They disappeared to the back of the church. Burt reappeared while the *Kyrie* was being sung. Five minutes later, the whirr of the high-power floor buffer penetrated the closed sanctuary doors.

I am one of those who prefer to sit in the back during service, in case I have to sneak out for a teeny-weeny bladder break. At the sound of the buffer, I flew through the doors, hit a spot where Ernie had poured liquid polish and finished the last ten feet to the whining machine looking like a Jane Fonda exercise video on fast forward. Ernie caught me under the arms as I madly slapped at the off switch.

"Are you nuts!" I hissed at him.

"I'm doing my community service," he calmly replied.

I stepped away from him, looking for a dull linoleum escape route. "During church services? Don't you have any other time you can work?"

Ernie moved the buffer against the wall. "Not this week. I'm being more productive for this church than all the people sitting in the next room."

Rather than stumble down the thorny path of direct confrontation, I said, "You know, you'll be right back in court if some parishioner slips on this floor." I grabbed the stack of industrial-strength towels that served as napkins for the dessert table and went down on my knees.

"Don't, Anna," Ernie said. "You're in a nice dress." He got down on one knee beside me and began wiping up the polish.

"I have no idea what some church or church member did to make you like you are," I said, trying to maintain my composure, "and I'm fairly certain you won't share it with me. But my church will not become an outlet for your wrath."

The doors opened. Burt's bewildered face came through.

"It's okay," I assured. "Don't miss the readings."

Burt vanished. Ernie sighed.

Every year on Memorial Day weekend, the Skytop Road folk participate in an advertised block flea market. For days before the event, we bargain with and threaten our husbands to let go of their "but it's *good* crap" that has been gathering dust in attics, basements and closets. We negotiate with our kids to let them keep the money gotten for Transformers, Easy-Bake Ovens, Beanie Babies and million-piece Lego sets they have been holding onto like baby teeth. My personal responsibility is to collect the atrocities presented to us by relatives and friends for birthdays, holidays and anniversaries, and to cull through the bookshelves to make room for new murder mysteries. After fighting off the professional bargain hunters who duck walk under the garage door as it is rising and after spending four more hours sitting in the sun grinning at even stranger strangers, I turn what collectively cost more than two thousand bucks at Bed, Bath and Beyond, Macy's, Barnes and Noble, Fashion Bug and Toys"R"Us into a total profit of thirty-nine dollars and twenty-five cents (less the money the kids and the husband use to buy other neighbors' junk).

Not everyone participates every year, of course. Ernie Love had not participated the previous year and showed no sign of it this one either. This was duly noted to me by Hugh as he took his obligatory stroll up and down the street, like Patton reviewing the troops. For some reason, his chapeau of choice was always a surplus World War II pith helmet from the Army Air Corps, which he wore with a white handkerchief tucked under the back to keep the sun off his neck. His words about Ernie were studiously nonchalant as he examined a souvenir Terminator mug my son had picked up at Universal Studios theme park years before and had insisted someone would buy.

"This is nice," Hugh admired. "Where's the snap-on top and

built-in straw?" He was clearly a canny connoisseur of such memorabilia.

"Must be lost," I said, expecting that he would put the old thing down.

Hugh held onto the mug, rearing back his lips to show his teeth to the red-eyed endoskeleton figure on the side. "I had a brilliant idea, Anna. You know we've earned a lot of publicity for our street over the years from our Christmas decorating. Then Dr. Strangelove pushed us right over the top with his dead deer. I figure it's time to take advantage of our fame, negative and positive, and kick it up a notch."

I asked him what kind of notch he wanted to kick.

"Charge every carload that comes through to see the displays. How much you want for this mug?"

Liam had set the price at a quarter. Liking Hugh as much as I did, I told him, "My son and that were inseparable, but he's willing to part with it for a buck. You can't charge people for driving on a public road, Hugh."

"Oh, it will be purely voluntary. But who's gonna be stingy when the event has been covered in the local papers and on the radio? Who's gonna say no to little kids with drippy, red noses standing out in the cold holding Mason jars we prime with cash? Who's got a heart small enough not to be touched when we collect for Goodwill?" His eyes grew big. "Get it? 'The Goodwill Society'? And we publicize it as 'Good Will to Men'!"

"Sounds pretty calculating to me, Hugh," I responded.

He smiled. "Yeah. Thanks."

"Have you contacted the Society yet?"

"You think they're gonna object to trading their name for cold cash?" He laughed. "Cold cash. Pretty funny, eh?"

"They might," I warned.

"Nah. Everyone will play along. Even The-Grinch-in-Disguise Ernest Love can't refuse to join in on a charity event."

"And what if he does refuse?" I asked.

Hugh grinned like Sylvester with Tweety Bird in his paws. "Then hundreds of people, maybe thousands, will see what an ungodly, un-American bedbug he is. Are you sure you don't have the top to this mug?"

"Nope."

"What about the straw?"

"Sorry."

Hugh dug into his pocket. "I'll take it anyway. You'll be getting a flier announcing a street meeting on the event next week." He smiled even more broadly. "Everybody will."

CHAPTER FOUR

HE NEVER MENTIONED how he had done it, but Ernie Love somehow found and installed critical replacement parts that would allow our ancient church boiler to limp along for another few years. He also got the toilets to stop backing up. Pastor Hartmann reported that Ernie did the work on consecutive Wednesday afternoons. Work that needed doing in the church kitchen and dining area or in the narthex, however, he tended to exclusively on Sunday mornings. There were the stained ceiling tiles from the Great Flood of 2000 (no rainbow was reported afterward), the moldy molding that needed repainting, the electrical outlets too loose to hold plugs, the loose notice board, the slow drip in the kitchen sink, the cranky sink light that needed a new ballast resistor, the low spot under the tile floor. All of it had needed "eventual attention," but somehow the eventualities had never happened before Ernie arrived.

The kitchen, dining and narthex areas were the heart of activities before and between services. From there, Ernie could see and hear virtually everything that went on. I noticed that his work slowed in proportion to his interest in each particular event. The couple of times I ran out to the bathroom, I had also caught him hanging near the doors to the sanctuary during the pastor's sermons. He began to remind me of that solitary bag of animated fur that hung around the trooper's outpost in *Dances With Wolves.*

Most Sundays, between services, the pastor holds an adult study session. Because of St. Mark's symbol and because two frequenters graduated from Penn State, the group calls itself The Litany Lions. Truth be known, it's not a fierce den of liturgical or theological debate. The usual topic is the gospel reading for that day, and those in the group behave more like sheep. One day in early February the reading was from Matthew 7 and contained the passage "Ask, and it will be given you; seek, and you will find; knock, and it will be opened to you. For every one who asks receives, and he who seeks finds, and to him who knocks it will be opened." I sat in the group, along with Jack and Marnie Frieden, Sally Wentworth, Morton Finch and Mimi Jacquard. The sitting area was smaller than usual, because the chairs and sofa had been pushed together to clear space from the baseboards moldings Ernie was painting. Mimi read the passage. Pastor Hartmann asked for comment, and before anyone in the circle could respond, Ernest Love's voice sounded from behind and below the couch.

"It's not true."

That was the whole of it. Three words if you count the contraction as one.

Everyone but the pastor looked surprised. Without much pause, he returned, "Never?"

"Yes, never."

"I've had my prayers answered plenty of—" Jack began defending with spirit.

Jeremiah Hartmann held up his hand for silence. He stared at the sofa as if he could peer through it to Ernie's face.

"You sound quite sure, Mr. Love."

"I am."

"You won't even admit to *some* petitions to God being answered?"

There was the sound of movement, and then Ernie appeared, crawling around the side of the sofa, his narrow brush held high. "Some things that people ask God for do happen, of course. But that's because they would have happened anyway. The farmer hasn't had rain for twenty days. He prays for it. The next day it rains. He thanks God for listening to him. If he hadn't prayed, it would have rained anyway. Pure statistical probability."

"Wait a minute!" Jack said, as he swung around to face Ernie. "I had a biopsy test for prostate cancer that the doctor said turned my prostate temporarily into Swiss cheese. The results came back from the lab as positive. Big-time positive. Because of the biopsy, I was told I couldn't be operated on for six weeks, until the prostate had healed up. Otherwise it would have fallen apart, and some of the cancer cells might have fallen into the healthy ones. Now, I want the best prostate surgeon in the country if I can get him. So I pray. My wife prays. The church members pray. Jewish and Muslim friends pray. Lo and behold, the guy working in the same office as my wife has just has his prostate taken out by the country's Number One surgeon. Down at Johns Hopkins. Miracle One. We get on the visit list five times faster than normal. When we meet the surgeon, he agrees that the prostate has to come out. But he's in such demand that he can't operate on me for five months. I tell him I can't wait that long. He says he'll check with his secretary. While he's gone, I say another prayer. A minute later he walks into the room with a strange look on his face.

"'When's the earliest your physician told you that you could be operated on?' he asked me. I told him 'July third.' He said, 'While I was standing there waiting to talk with my nurse, she hung up the phone and said the guy scheduled for July third just cancelled. Almost no one cancels on me.'" Jack smiled down at Ernie. "'Ask and it shall be given.'"

Ernie stood. "Luck. If it wasn't luck, all the millions praying for peace would have been heard and answered. No son would die in battle. Nobody would starve to death. No patient would die of cancer. I gotta wash this brush."

I do not need to tell you that Ernie had knocked over the proverbial hornet's nest. After he calmed the circle, Pastor Hartmann's wisdom was that Jesus did not talk in mild terms. When he said that if your eye offended you, he really didn't want you to blind yourself. Rather, he wanted you to think seriously about your actions. Similarly, for those who relied solely on themselves, Jesus was saying that they needed to turn to the Lord more. The same Lord who provided the land and seeds for crops, and animals to tame, and stone and wood and clay for shelter. If two sides both prayed to God to win a contest, well, that was clearly not possible. God heard all prayers and, in some way, answered them all. But the answer was not necessarily what the petitioner wanted to hear.

Ernie Love had no reply, since he had excused himself and did not return. I must say that the gospel scripture passage had given me pause. Ernie merely had the nerve to say what many of us were too polite or scared to bring out in the open. My fear of trouble from Ernie fulfilling his community service at St. Mark's was coming true.

CHAPTER FIVE

TWICE A YEAR, between Sunday services, we hold a congregational meeting. February is the more important of the two forums, because the budget is presented and voted on. As with almost every other main line denomination church in our part of the country, the size of the congregation has been steadily shrinking. Three-fifths of all young folk are turning fully to the worship of Self, using Sundays for organized sports, shopping for all the must-have stuff marketed at them or vegging out after a Saturday night of hard partying. Another fifth have dropped their parents' churches in favor of charismatic groups that make religion into entertainment. The devil in pleasing shapes and the feel-good-about-yourself-while-giving-a-passing-nod-to-God churches are hard competition. When my husband and I had joined St. Mark's nineteen years earlier, the average weekly attendance was 108. The year just lapsed had averaged 82. Dire handwriting on the wall is not confined merely to the Old Testament.

Rich Parker, the current council president, read aloud the most important figures of the proposed budget, a copy of which had been handed to each attendee. He finished by saying, "The good news is that unit giving is almost unanimously up across the membership. The bad news is that it still doesn't meet inflation. Furthermore, four families moved out of the area and only two new ones joined last year. Also, three long-time contributors passed to eternal joy."

As church president, Rich had the euphemisms down pat. Before he could ask for comment, John Whitworth, the church's self-appointed old curmudgeon, croaked, "So, cut out items or cut back salaries."

We had wrangled over his same two suggestions for the past three years. When it came to skillful carving, we had already cut to the bone. Pastor Hartmann had not had a raise in two years. Our church secretary's hours had been halved. The custodial line had already been eliminated.

Morton Finch, who was very proud of his basso profundo voice and who had head resonance where more brains might have served him better, asked, "What happened to our renting the parking lot out to the roller blading school?"

"That was five years ago, Morty. Roller blading is out of vogue," Mimi Jacquard informed. "Besides, that idea cost us an insurance increase when that kid fell and broke his arm. Remember?"

Morty snapped his fingers and nodded.

Betty Burroughs said, "It's been three years since our last flea market and bake sale. Shouldn't we try that again?"

"You think the community's memory is that short?" Linda Black responded, tactfully refraining from mentioning Ida Clark's name.

Ida was one of the three church members who had died the previous year. Three years earlier, the poor lady was farther into dementia than we had suspected. Her non-member son always dropped her off just before church began and picked her up directly afterward. Ida had not sung the hymns and rarely recited the liturgy in her good years, so her blank staring throughout the service truly looked no different than the decades when she was "with it." Nor was she a regular attendee of any extra-worship activity except the bake and cook sales. How were we to know, we absolved each other afterward.

For the fundraising event, Ida had cooked up a huge crockpot of chili con carne. The informal jury of inquiry figured she must have left the chopped meat out on the counter for a few days before putting it in the pot. I was told by the victims that it tasted fine. But its affect on digestive tracts was something terrible. Within an hour, it was cleaning people out both ends like Roto Rooter. I can only imagine the mishaps of strangers who had scavenged through our fleas and then lunched in the St. Mark's parking lot that day. Surely some of them had then driven to other errands, well out of range of known rest stops. The church's overtaxed toilets, which were sorely needed by the half dozen parishioners who worked at tables that day and who had bought Ida's chili, predictably backed up. We tried to put a lid on the crockpot scandal, so to speak, but several sufferers in the community insisted on making a big stink and the *Bunhouse Beacon* got wind of it, to release two more clichés.

Lest you think from my tattling that I'm a naturally harsh and judgmental person or that our church is stocked to the rafters with life's walking wounded, I must let you know that John, Morton and Ida have perennially been our three most eccentric characters. Three out of one hundred and eighty-six on the rolls ain't bad. Every organization has its share, and since we are assured that God loves and embraces everyone, no restrictions whatsoever on membership can be permitted. I heartily concur. However, this does create its moments.

"Let's try the flea market – *without* the baking and cooking," Rich suggested. The notion was approved.

"What about bidding earlier in the year for the heater oil?" Burt piped up.

"What about installing solar panels?" another voice asked before anyone could reply to Burt's words.

The voice was unfamiliar to most. It also came from the back doorway into the sanctuary. Everyone turned.

Ernest Love stood with his arms folded, as if he had been listening for quite some time.

"This meeting is for church members," John Whitworth declared in his raspy, curmudgeon voice.

"How about allowing comment from those who make contributions to the church?" Ernie countered, already reaching for his wallet. "I could give you a list of the tasks I've finished, and you can tell me how many men at St. Mark's have done as much in the past year."

"That's not–" John bristled.

But Ernie was not finished. He walked down the center aisle toward the collection plates, which normally would have been carried to the business office by this time but were still resting near the altar due to the meeting. His fingers dug into his wallet. "Yes, I know," he interrupted. "It's rude stating the obvious. But if my work the past few weeks hasn't been enough to allow me to talk, perhaps my money will be. Here's fifty dollars to help your budget shortfall."

While Ernie deposited the money, a soft murmur ran through the membership.

"Solar panels cost a fortune to install," Jack Frieden declared in a dismissing tone.

"They are expensive," Ernie allowed, "but much cheaper if they're self-installed."

"Who has that kind of skill?" Jack asked.

"I do," Ernie answered.

The murmuring rose and fell again.

"The church won't get a tax rebate, but solar energy will pay for itself in savings within five years." Ernie had started back toward the rear of the sanctuary, but he stopped when he got within a couple feet of Jack. "What you have to ask yourselves is, 'Will this church be open in five years?' Well…will it?" The cocking of his head and narrowing of his eyes looked a lot like Dirty Harry's.

I expected somebody to reply, if not to shout him down. But I was naïve. The question was more than fair and had no doubt come into the minds of anyone who had worshiped in the numerous services that contained fewer than thirty others. Ernest Love used the silence to continue. From behind his wire-rim glasses, his still-narrowed eyes swept the assemblage.

"According to the annual report, your average number of service attendees went down by four over the previous year. I'm sure this church had at least twenty more families attending ten years ago. Now, I'm not a religious man, but I do know that Jesus asked only a few things of those who believe in him: Love God with all your heart; love your neighbors as yourself; and go into all the world and preach the good word to every creature. I won't embarrass you about the first two. Have you at least done the last one?"

"Of course we have!" Morty asserted. "I spend one Sunday afternoon every month knocking on doors."

"Good for you, sir. Has everyone in this room done the same?" Ernie asked. "An article in the local paper last year said that only one in five families in this county now attends church regularly."

"And you're among the other four," the curmudgeon shot back.

"Guilty as charged," Ernie admitted. He looked at me. "In spite of Anna doing her subtle best to get me here. I'm not saying you'll get everyone. I'm not saying you'll get one in a hundred. But you only need, what, a dozen more members to be back in good shape? What does it say in Matthew? 'Seek, and ye shall find; knock, and it shall be opened unto you.'"

Now, I was at that moment reflecting on the new clue that Ernest Love could install a solar panel system by himself. At that same moment, I'm pretty sure at least half the rest of the people in the sanctuary were thinking, "Who is this guy who won't belong to a church, yet not only knows scripture but can tell you what book it's from?" I figured Ernie had remembered the passage from the recent session where he had claimed God did not answer prayers. But only seven of us were there at the time. For the rest of the congregation, the quotation was like a royal robe Ernie had suddenly clothed himself in. It gave him authority that had to be respected.

Rich told Ernie, "In the past five years we tried a thousand-call telephone campaign, a blitz of large ads in the newspaper, a new sign board out front and a contemporary service with a soft rock band."

"And the annual Living Nativity," I reminded him.

"And the annual Living Nativity," he repeated. "I think that's a good amount of seeking. By my count, all these efforts yielded three new members…beyond those new residents who sought us out."

"Okay. Three more than none," Ernie said. He removed his spectacles and smiled at the congregation. "But what about the 'Knock, and it shall be opened to you'? I tell you what. Even though I am not a member of your church, if you will pledge to collectively spend two hundred hours knocking on doors in the next two months, I will add another twenty hours to my community service helping you."

Rich looked around the sanctuary. Everyone else looked around as well. Faces were positive. The affect of Dirty Harry transforming back to smiling Ernest Love was infectious. Heads began to nod.

"Deal!" Rich replied.

30

CHAPTER SIX

AS I COULD have predicted, most of Skytop Road liked Hugh's idea of holiday fundraising by assaulting carloads of gawkers. As I also knew would happen, Ernie Love flatly refused to be part of the neighborhood light show. The general opinion on the street was as Hugh had intended. Ernie was unofficially, as my husband likes to say, persona au gratin. Whenever I was given the opportunity – during dog-walking encounters or at the grocery store, for example – I defended his stance and informed neighbors of the good he was doing at St. Mark's. Many listened, but several were not interested in having their opinion altered by facts.

Alienating Dr. Love, however, was not enough by half for Hugh. Although it could not be proven, he had several times called local realtors, identified himself as Ernie, and asked them to stop by his house in anticipation of selling it. Whenever Hugh's metrosexual offspring, the bass guitarist for a heavy metal rock band that had been for years "on the edge of stardom," came home from tours, Hugh had Jessie park his/her rust-ridden Nissan van in front of Ernie's house. Chimney sweeps and plumbers knocked on his front door at all hours answering phony emergency calls.

I had seen all of this traffic out my windows through the winter, but I did not have the opportunity to question Ernie about it until mid-March, when I met him in the Bunhouse Cumberland Farms convenience store. I had passed Hugh's St. Patrick's Day display only minutes before, and his one-way feud with Ernie was on my mind. It was difficult not to think of Hugh many times each year, in fact, no matter how much one tried: holidays provided the perfect excuse to call indirect attention to himself. The day after he took down his Christmas extravaganza, up went the Valentine's display. It featured oversized red, heart-shaped candles in every window – except the one in his living room, where a four-foot illuminated heart pulsed as if beating. A flag with multi-colored hearts hung from his porch post. From lawn speakers, the sounds of "Love Will Keep Us Together" played on an endless loop. His mailbox was wrapped in red foil. On the lawn, a six-foot-high inflated heart with an equally inflated arrow through it was held aloft by tandem inflated cherubs. On February 15th, the red was replaced by green, with inflatable leprechauns cavorting on the lawn, a flag with Brian Boru's harp, a giant glitter rainbow ending in a cauldron and paper shamrocks taped over every window. Predictably, the mailbox was wrapped in green, iridescent paper. The song perpetually pulsing through lower Skytop Road was "When Irish Eyes Are Smiling."

Visions of giant painted eggs and cavorting rabbits the size of Harvey danced in my head as I entered the Cumberland Farms. Ernie was buying the *New York Times*.

"Any more chimney sweeps show up?" I asked.

He tucked the paper under his arm. "No, but just in case, I went up on the roof and posted a sign saying nobody is to clean the chimney unless they see me first in person."

I verbally deplored the Illumination Mafia's petty tactics.

"It's okay. What comes 'round goes 'round," Ernie said, followed by his slightly crooked smile. Right then I knew that he had things in hand and that I need not worry on his behalf.

I picked up the rolls I had forgotten to buy at Wegman's supermarket and got in line behind Ernie. While he was checking out, Frieda Hoffmann walked into the place. Frieda is one of the stalwarts of the neighborhood. She lives around the corner from Skytop Road. Over the years, she has babysat numerous kids and seen that they got off to school and back home safely. She's the organizer of the Neighborhood Watch and the person responsible for the petition that got us upgraded power transformers. She assembles the annual Halloween Parade, etc., etc. I introduced her to Ernie and praised her efforts. They spoke briefly. He evaded her polite inquiries about his life in his gentle, but efficient, way.

When Ernie left, Frieda and I lingered outside the store.

"He's from the Midwest," Frieda pronounced, watching Ernie's purple Volvo pull away.

"Really?"

"I ought to know. I'm from the Midwest. In fact, he's from Southern Illinois, Missouri, Iowa, Kansas or Nebraska. Not Arkansas. Not Michigan, Minnesota, Indiana or the Dakotas. And not gone that long, I'd say. He definitely grew up around there."

I had no reason to doubt Frieda. She had a degree in linguistics from the University of Iowa. She immediately changed the subject, but my mind had now tucked away Easter bunnies and Kaiser rolls and was fixating once more on the mystery of Ernest Love.

The Internet may be filled with garbage – but for those who know how to use it, the invention is like having the Library of Congress in a box. The moment I got home I rushed to my computer. In the course of my many journalistic research projects, I have assembled the names of all of the major and many minor newspapers around the great U. S. of A. I called up my list and began scouring electronic Midwest newspaper morgues for the name E*** Love.

About an hour later, I hit paydirt. It seemed that two years earlier, a certain Edward Love, who was a Methodist preacher in Missouri with a Doctor of Divinity degree, lost his pulpit over a scandal. His church closed ranks and refused to go public with particulars. The article I read suggested that the reason was alienation of affections. To me, that meant he had seduced one or more church wives. Bespectacled Ernie certainly did not look like a Don Juan and I had never caught the hint of a lothario nature, but you know what they say: Still water turns into grain alcohol. Like psychiatrists, ministers have positions of authority and often gain the trust of persons they counsel. All too often, articles about priests seducing choirboys or pastors diverting church funds for vacations abroad prove that men of God have the same clay feet (or worse) as the rest of us. Much seemed to add up. Ernie had moved to our neighborhood about three months after the Edward Love scandal broke. Ernie was unwilling to speak about his past. Judge Cassato had called him "Doctor" and said that he had never been arrested for anything major. Most of all, Ernie was down on religion, or at least the organized variety. Even though he could quote the Bible with the best of them.

I felt no triumph as I shut down my computer.

34

CHAPTER SEVEN

I AM NO chemist, but I do know there are such things as catalysts. When introduced to otherwise inert chemicals, they compel all kinds of reactions and interesting, new compounds. Ernie Love was St. Mark's catalyst. I personally think it was his demonstrated non-believer status that spurred so many of us to revitalize our community evangelism and prove the power of faith at work. Fully thirty-one of our number signed up for door-to-door duty and received our individual recruitment grids. When I tell you that I dislike door knocking from both sides, believe me. I don't answer the Jehovah's Witnesses even if I have left the front door open. I instruct the environmentalist lobby college students to leave their literature on the doorstep through the safety of two inches of oak. For me to be the knocker, something extraordinary has to be happening. Of course, Ernie is my next-door neighbor, and I felt responsible for his presence at my church. Nevertheless, playing the Innkeeper's Wife in the annual Living Nativity is usually the limit to my witnessing for the Lord. And yet I trod boldly onto ninety-six private properties and rapped loudly or rang doorbells several times. Forty doors opened to me. Twenty-one people were cordial. Nineteen accepted my very inviting literature. Three even asked a couple questions. I ended up feeling good about my efforts. But nobody in my territory ever showed up later at St. Mark's.

At the other extreme, Ernest Love produced three "units" within three weeks. The first was a family: a mother, a father, and two boys. The second was a mother and two girls. The third was a solitary young woman who looked to be about twenty-four years old. The first seven visitors were Black. The young woman was Latina.

Ernie had managed to produce at St. Mark's a reaction equivalent to my neighborhood's reaction over the dead reindeer on his front lawn. Up until this point, our church had been Easter lily white. It sat physically in the middle of an upper middle-class residential area where the few Black families living there attended the AME or Baptist churches. I cannot remember until that month any discussions about race or ethnicity, because as far as St. Mark's was concerned the world might have contained nothing but pink-skinned people of European descent. From the registry sign-in, it was clear that all three sets of visitors came from Ashton, the town on Bunhouse's southern border, where the standard of living was considerably lower.

The reaction among the congregation was mixed. About half were color-blind and hastened up to the visitors before and after the service, helping them with the hymnals and bulletins, leading them to the cakes and coffee, making polite inquiries. Afterward, those members talked among themselves of nothing but the opportunity to add new souls to our "community of saints." Several members volunteered to drive to the visitors' homes with the day's altar flowers and one of the cinnamon spice loafs we keep frozen in the hopes of such rare occasions. Most of the other worshipers were silent about the turn of events, keeping their thoughts to themselves. A few had increasing trouble disguising their consternation at this threatened change in complexion of the congregation. These few said nothing for the first weeks, hoping in vain that the visitors would see none of "their kind" in the church and not literally darken our door again.

Mr. and Mrs. Ned Sharpe and their boys Nate and Omar returned the following Sunday. So did former Louisiana native Henrietta Fowler and her girls, Elisa and Orlene. After four weeks of visits, the Sharpes declared their intention of joining St. Mark's. The Fowlers followed suit two weeks later. Veteran members were pleased as punch when Mr. Sharpe revealed that he worked for a corporate landscape design company. As soon as the grass started growing again, he was out piloting a lawn mower the size of a small flying saucer, making short work of a job that had previously kept two members trudging behind mowers for an hour each. In the summer, he trucked in half a dozen azaleas and several ferns left over from a job. With large rocks and mounds of pine mulch, he transformed our front entry into something truly beautiful. Mrs. Fowler turned out to be a wizard in the kitchen. I suggested to Pastor Hartmann that if he wanted to increase attendance on certain Sundays all he needed to do was change the front sign message to "Henrietta Fowler's muffins following 8:30 service."

These contributions to St. Mark's did not seem to matter

much to some of the older members. After an April service, one at which no persons of dark skin had attended, Morty Finch starting asking around, "Who knocked on doors in Ashton? Who wasted their time? Everybody knows those people have no money. What was the point?"

Pastor Hartmann moved quickly to do damage control. "The point of evangelizing should not be the budget," he said loudly. "God does not need our money for His will to be done."

Morton's thick, black eyebrows elevated in surprise. "Oh, yeah? Maybe not in heaven. But down here, everything survives on the Almighty buck. I'm sure you're not refusing your salary, Pastor. You must know who went down to Ashton."

"It's not important," the pastor said.

John Whitworth waddled arthritically up to the conversation. "Don't be dense, Mort. It could only be one troublemaker: Ernie Love. All you had to do was ask one of them." "Them" meant the pledging members.

"Did *you* ask?" Morty wanted to know.

"You bet I did. Of course it was him. The atheist is doing what he can to wreck the church from the inside."

I saw Leonard Carrington turning red with anger. Leonard is a good Christian soul, but turning the cheek for himself or on the behalf of others is not his forté. I waded in before he could reduce the discussion to a shouting match.

"Exactly how is the church being wrecked from the inside, John?" I asked.

He smirked at me. "Right away, by filling the pews with people who won't pull their load financially. Later, by changing worship. The first thing you know, we'll be listening to 'Amens' and 'Preach it, brother' from the seats. Then, we'll be swaying and clapping to the hymns. Then who knows what else."

"I'm telling you if there are Blacks and Mexicans in heaven," Morty declared, "I don't think I want to be there."

The pastor moved past the two men toward his study. "I don't think you'll have to worry about it, Morton."

I thought about asking the pair rhetorically how much it cost the church for warm bodies to sit in empty pews, but I knew my sarcasm would only cause them to fortify their positions. On the subject of how the new people came to the church, John Whitworth could not be debated. Without formally signing up for a territory or consulting anyone at St. Mark's, Ernest Love had taken it upon himself to canvas a major section of Ashton. I caught him in his driveway the Monday after the narthex blow-up.

"Why didn't you tell anyone you were recruiting for St. Mark's in Ashton?" I asked him, point blank.

"I said in the meeting that I would add twenty hours to my community service," he replied.

"Everybody assumed you meant by working around the church."

"Everybody assumed wrong."

"And why Ashton?" I pushed.

"Because it makes the most sense. Your previous phone campaign was confined to the Bunhouse area. Morton Finch only knocks on doors in Bunhouse. Ashton was completely untapped."

"You had no ulterior motives?" I asked archly.

"What motives would those be?"

"Were there African Americans and Latinos in your church in the Midwest?" I countered, watching carefully for a chink in his expressionless expression.

Ernie slowly broke into his crooked smile. "Unfortunately, there weren't. I suppose you could call that one of my motives."

"Well, whatever your motives are," I assured him, "you did a good thing."

"How did you learn that I came from the Midwest?" he asked.

I told him what Frieda Hoffmann had said at the Cumberland Farms. "Now you owe me the answer to a question that's been bugging me for months. Since you don't have a family, why did you buy such a large house? Why not a condo or townhouse?"

"First of all, I come from wide open spaces. I can't stand the idea of sharing walls with strangers and having to listen to their arguments and loud music. Secondly, a large house appreciates faster than a small one." Ernie proceeded to tell me in detail how houses were among the few possessions that gained rather than lost value over time. He then went into how, over the years, you paid off the house only on the value of its purchase price even as it appreciated and that normal inflation made the payback cheaper every year. I was so astonished at the quantity of words that poured out of him that I could not bring myself to confess that I already knew everything he was telling me. His enthusiasm was so obvious that I found it impossible to believe he was relating anything but the truth, the whole truth, and nothing but the truth.

It was several states removed from the whole truth.

You must have noticed that I have written nothing about the Latina woman after first mentioning her. Her name was Lucia Rodriguez. She was more than pretty, with long, black, shiny hair that she kept in pigtails, rosy cheeks, generous lips, large brown eyes, and an excellent figure that she chose to conceal under formless shifts. Nor did she wear high heels to elevate her diminutive figure.

Because Lucia was so easy to look at *and* had no children in tow *and* sang on key *and* spoke English without an accent, she caught our church's self-appointed Border Patrol off guard. Nothing she said or did hinted that Lucia Rodriguez would cause an uproar at St. Mark's. She sat demurely, recited, and sang just like the White folks. She also placed a five-dollar bill in the offering plate each Sunday. No one could count this newcomer from the other side of the tracks as a liability.

There was one temporary problem with Lucia. The first week she attended, she sat on the left side, second row from the back, far left seat. No one remembered to inform her that, although no warning had been posted anywhere, this was Augusta Rettig's seat. Augusta, well into her seventies, had of late begun attending church only every other week. She also never arrived earlier than ten minutes into the service. The Confession of Sins, *Introit, Kyrie,* and *Gloria* were no longer of interest to her, she having heard the same liturgy since Martin Luther was a teenager. From my back seat on the left side, I had a perfect view of the moment. The rest of the congregation droned the zombie version of "Glory to God in the highest" as Choirmaster Fields flailed his arms around, exhorting the sopranos and altos to more volume. Augusta doddered right up to the edge of the pew before she realized her space had been violated. She took several more steps, pivoted, folded her arms across her shriveled chest, cocked her right eyebrow, and glared in silence at Lucia. Lucia understood almost immediately and slid down the pew to the middle. One mercy from a church with dwindling numbers is all the empty pew space.

That same March and April, the canvassing efforts of our member legion of shoe-leather evangelists produced two families from the Bunhouse community (one lasting only until the summer sports season). A young couple, newly moved in, also chose our church as their spiritual home. Happy days were here again. God was still in his heaven. All seemed right with the St. Mark's world.

Need I point out the verb in the last sentence?

CHAPTER EIGHT

EACH YEAR, ON the weekend before Memorial Day, our church holds a calendar party. The purpose is ostensibly for fundraising. The only problem is that those who attend are almost all members of the church. If you host a table, you end up spending about a week's salary and a week's time in preparations. It would be far easier for the participants to increase their yearly contribution by another few hundred dollars. If it wasn't for our national Lutheran benevolent society matching the proceeds, I'd militate – with a weapon if necessary – for dropping the event.

Here's how it works. Twelve victims pick their favorite month and decorate a table for eight with an appropriate theme. Then she (no male has ever volunteered in eight years of this idea from hell) pays for her family to attend, even though she's already paid for everything else. Then she calls in favors from her relatives. If the places still aren't filled, she lies to her friends about how great it will be. They're not fooled, and she resorts to begging and reminding them how many Girl Scout cookies she has bought from them over the years. She shops for the decorations. Then she buys a door prize. Then she plans the meal. Then she takes off the Friday afternoon of the thing to shop for the food, decorate her table, and cook the food. Then she hosts the meal and again cajoles people to buy tickets, this time to vote on whose table and fare are best. Then she cleans up for two hours – a task I like to call the aftermath. Fun, huh? There are several ladies at St. Mark's who actually revel in this torture. When it comes to entertaining, I would rather have a root canal. And I mean entertaining in the comfort of my own home.

So, the year of the big evangelism push I am "volunteered" for the calendar party by Mildred Hunsucker, who has been known to break into full-blown hysterics and openly question your attitude toward her as a human being if you pause to inhale before accepting. Since I didn't volunteer the day the party was announced, February,

March, July, November, and December – the easy ones – were already snatched up. So were April, May, June, and October. This left me with January, August, or September. For a while I contemplated "Taking a January Cruise," but, unlike me, cruise ships excel in their cuisine. I have been known to wreck Kraft Mac 'n Cheese. I settled on September and an Eagles theme. Crescendo's bakery makes a great football cake, right down to the Eagles insignia. I got a green tablecloth and created a gridiron from thin white masking tape. William and Liam made goalposts for me. The Party Store has football figures that my boys carefully set up into the Eagles versus the Giants on either side of a halftime show platform they had also built. The show featured a miniature rock band and a male and female vocalist. Underneath, our old cassette tape recorder played "Fly, Eagles, Fly," the theme from *Rocky*, and other appropriate tunes. No fool I, my fare was hotdogs, cheese fries, beer, and sodas in our accumulated Eagles plastic schooners. Little inverted helmets with frozen Dippin' Dots sufficed for the dessert. All three of the Morn clan wore Eagles sweatshirts.

At any normal church, my table might have had a fighting chance at winning. But when Lutherans get into something, it's the hog from snout to squiggly tail. The table in front of me, "June Wedding," featured Lenox china, antique Paul Revere flatware, Waterford crystal stemware, and linen cloths. The bouquet in the middle of the table looked more like a Tournament of Roses float. The hostess wore a wedding dress. Every place had a disposable camera. The dessert was a three-tier wedding cake. The guests had their choice of chicken Florentine, stuffed flounder, or filet mignon. The table behind mine, "April in Paris," had a four-foot-high replica of the Eiffel Tower built from two Erector sets as its centerpiece. The fare was coq au vin, truffles, pommes frites, and French-cut green beans. The choice of wine was a Lafitte Rothschild or a Châteauneuf du Pape. The dessert was Crêpes Suzette with Dom Perignon. Everyone got his or her own beret. The hostess hired a mime. Our table got seventeen votes. I paid for fifteen of them.

Even if I had hired two members of the Eagles' offensive backfield for the evening, I still wouldn't have won. I was busy in the kitchen boiling my hot dogs while my son was scandalizing most of the attendees. Unbeknownst to me, he had engineered a wardrobe malfunction for the female figure atop their halftime show. That lost me the coveted trophy. That and the fact that Henrietta Fowler's

March theme was "Mardi Gras." Her centerpiece was two authentic fancy masks from way back when New Orleans had just replaced Mobile as the Mardi Gras capital. Brightly-colored beaded necklaces made her table shine. She had old Blues and Ragtime sheet music under glassine as placemats. A mix CD her girls had prepared featured Winton Marsalas, Al Hirt and Louis Armstrong belting out Dixieland. But her food was the hurricane that blew everyone else's extravaganza away. She started with puffy-light beignets, and then intensified to the gale force winds of killer gumbo and jambalaya with red beans and rice. Just to make sure the competition was completely flattened, she added a tornado key lime pie. Not the green stuff restaurants up North serve but the delicate yellow-hued variety that tastes like a wedge from a heavenly cloud. As you might have guessed, I sampled more from Henrietta's table than from my own.

The fact that Henrietta should have won notwithstanding, it was gratifying to see so many members of the congregation voting for a newcomer. That made the evening special. But regarding specials, the formal contest only took fourth place.

Third place went to Morton Finch. For years, he had pestered self-appointed, calendar-party-dictator-for-life Mildred Hunsucker to provide the after-dinner entertainment. Mildred, however, had seen Morton in action the year he was allowed to play Wise Man Number One in our vaunted outdoor Living Nativity. Director George Reeder, who usually insists that no one who isn't off script by the last rehearsal can go on, fatally bowed to Mort's solemn promise on a Bible that he would have his speeches down by opening night. I can understand why George folded. The part, after all, only had a few lines: "Oh great Potentate, where is he who has been born king of the Jews? For we have seen his star in the East and have come to worship him." Then, when Herod asks him where the Christ is to be born, he replies, "In Bethlehem in the land of Judea; for so it is written by the prophets: 'And you, O Bethlehem, in the land of Judah, are by no man least among the rulers of Judah; for from you shall come a ruler who will govern my people Israel.'" Something anyone could memorize, given six weeks. You would think.

The cue for the Wise Men's entry is verse three of "We Three Kings." Morty plunged into the light in the middle of verse one, compelling the other two actors to follow along. There they stood with nothing to do but clutch their treasure chests. Wise Men Two and Three pretended to be confused and to consult with each other.

Morty did not need to feign confusion. He consulted his watch, which he had neglected to remove. When he did, his frankincense fell out of his casket. He also stepped on his robe, which caused him to fly across the set directly in front of King Herod's throne, which fortunately had not yet been lit. From the audience, however, there was more than enough light to see Morty's sneakers. Because he had entered so early, he had plenty of time to wander back to his place. From there, he picked out members of his family in the audience and snuck them little waves.

Finally, the music ended and the lights went up. Morty forgot every direction George had given him. He stepped in front of Herod, blocking him from view. Then he faced the seated king and delivered his first lines upstage, his back to the audience. The average amateur actor among our group can barely be heard to the front row of seats out in the open night field next to the church. With back turned, nothing would have been heard. But Morton Finch's normal voice sounds like the "Attention K-Mart shoppers" guy. Every syllable was heard when he said, "Oh, Impotentate! Where is he who is born king of–." He stopped suddenly, finally registering Herod's forefinger wriggling in a circle. Poor, hidden Jack Frieden was doing his best to signal Morty to turn around. Morty figured Jack meant he was saying his line backward. "This king of the Jews…," he corrected, "Where exactly is he to be born?" His next line was completely forgotten. Our veteran Herod struggled out of his throne, grabbed Morty, twirled him around, and asked, "How do you know a king is to be born?"

"What?" Morty asked.

Jack's shoulders slumped visibly. "Did you see a sign in the heavens, or what?"

"Oh! Right. Yeah, we…these other two wise guys and I…saw a big star in the East." Morty jerked his thumb over his right shoulder. The Star of the East, which sat atop a thirty-foot-high pole at the back of the field, had been illuminated during "We Three Kings." It shone brightly over Morty's left shoulder.

Rapidly losing patience and desperate to save what was left of the performance, Jack strode over to Lewis Henderson, Wise Man Number Two, another veteran of the annual event. "*You* look like a wise man," Jack extemporized. "Can you tell me where this king is to be born?" At which point, Morty tapped him on the trailing shoulder and said, "No, that's my line, Herod. I have the answer. Are you ready? It's Bethlehem! You know..." And then he began singing "Oh, little town of Bethlehem..."

"I know the place," Jack assured, "it's in the land of Judah."

This sparked a faint memory in Morty's mind. "'For from you shall come a ruler who shall govern all of Israel.'" Convinced he had at least nailed the final sentence, Morty faced the audience, grinned, and wiggled his eyebrows up and down in triumph. Herod flung himself back onto his throne as the lights came down prematurely. The Finch family's raucous applause and whistling did not help matters.

Afterward, Morty was not in the least apologetic. "So what if my lines were a little different?" he told everyone he met. "It's not like they had a court stenographer there. My wise man could have said exactly what I said!"

But even disasters are eventually forgotten, and like the Biblical widow who waits at the judge's gate and wears him down with daily petitions, Morty managed at long last to wrangle the calendar party entertainment spot from Mildred.

A (large) part of my nature is perverse. I waited to see what Morty had devised like an only child panting for Christmas morning.

The entertainment was a Finch family affair. Jack Frieden later pronounced them the Von Crapp Family. Morty's younger brother, Dan, yodeled. Not the simple, Swiss variety. Dan professed to yodel arias from the classical repertoire. We were treated to "La Donna é Mobile," Figaro's "Largo al Factotum" and "Vesti la Giubba" from *I Pagliacci*. At least we were told as much. The tunes were unrecognizable. I personally thought he sounded like he was performing a self-castration.

Morty's wife, Maybelle, did battle with an accordion. And lost. Her first rendering, that old staple no accordionist is allowed to avoid, was "Lady of Spain." She got most of the notes right, even if she played it at one-quarter tempo. Having turned that lilting air into a dirge, I find it beyond reason why she would attempt as her second piece "The Flight of the Bumblebee." My husband later christened it "The Crawl of the Caterpillar."

Morty himself did card tricks, dressed in top hat and tails. Badly. The worst of it was that he used normal-sized playing cards, so nobody beyond the first two tables could tell if he was succeeding or not. The best part of his performance was his grandson. He also was known as Morty, even though his name was Mortimer, not Morton.

In stage whispers from the back of the room, Little Morty gave away the secret of every one of his grandfather's tricks. Up front, Big Morty labored to maintain a broad smile, even as he shot eye daggers at the boy and periodically called out, "No comments from the peanut gallery!" and "Maybelle, shut that kid up!"

But the piéce de resistance was Little Morty and his two-man crosscut saw. I don't know if you've ever seen one of these North Woods lumberjack tools, but they are huge. Way too large for a ten-year-old to control as a musical instrument. A knowledgeable, strong, skilled adult can sit on a chair, use his hands to control a double bass bow and the upper handle of the saw, and clamp the lower handle to the floor with his feet. By bending the saw up and down and drawing the bow back and forth along its smooth edge, eerie but interesting tunes can be played. Little Morty was not doing well.

I have to assume this dubious skill was introduced to Mortimer by his grandfather, because when he began to flag at "Twinkle, Twinkle Little Star," Big Morty rushed onto the stage from the wings and attempted to grab the top of the saw from in front. At that very moment, the floor that had been so well polished by Ernie Love caused the bottom of the saw to escape from under Little Morty's shoes. In that instant, he had been trying to produce a high note so that his pressure on the top of the saw was prodigious. Like a sprung mousetrap, the saw bounded up straight between Big Morty's wide-spread knees. The flying handle disappeared beyond his trouser legs, sending both wings of his tails flying outward as if he were taking off.

The saw clattered to the floor, making its first pretty notes of the evening. For several seconds, Morty stood rooted to the spot like an old oak. Then, also like an old oak, he toppled straight backward. On the way down, his fall was partially broken by a pair of cymbals from the church drum set. Their combined crash was a fitting accompaniment to the accident. And to the climax of the entertainment.

There is a good reason why I attend church. I need to. While some rushed to Morty's assistance and others cried out in dismay and concern, I started laughing. I grabbed my napkin and clapped it over my mouth, pretending to have experienced a sudden fit of coughing. My ruse might have worked had not Ernest Love, who sat right beside me, said, "La commedia é finita." I could not get out of the room fast enough to disguise my mirth. The lack of blood calmed most of the partiers down quickly. The saw-turned-instrument's teeth had been filed down so that Morty received nothing worse than shredded trousers, several deep scratches, and swollen private parts. As he was helped out to his car, his basso profundo voice sounded like that of a reedy tenor.

Right now you're asking yourself, "If all that only took third place among special events, what else could have happened at this calendar party?" I'll tell you.

Second place was Henrietta Fowler's invitation to Blanche Coleman and her son, Dontrelle, to attend the dinner. Their acceptance elevated the persons of color at the party above ten percent, something no member of St. Mark's would have imagined only weeks before. Blanche is Henrietta's cousin and neighbor. I have since grown quite close to Blanche. It turns out that she and I have the same evil sense of humor. When she stopped daubing at her eyes and fanning herself over Big Morty and the Saw, she announced on the spot that St. Mark's seemed like exactly the church family she had been looking for. And to think that I had for years been excoriating those churches who build their membership by entertaining!

In a way, second place went to Ernie Love. Without his knocking on doors in Ashton, ten persons of color would not have been at the dinner. Amazingly, our active non-member also took the evening's top prize. Ever since Lucia Rodriguez walked into St. Mark's he could not keep his eyes off her. Not that he did not try his best. He was simply the moth and she the flame. Up until her visit, Ernie had either listened to the service from the narthex when all the doors happened to be closed or otherwise ventured as far as the doorways. Once Lucia took her weekly seat in the middle of the next-to-last left row, he sat right beside me. From his vantage point, he could catch an angled view of her pretty profile. Week after week after week.

When Lucia first showed at the church, I and others I spoke with assumed that Ernie had recruited her right along with the Fowlers and the Sharpes. However, unlike those families, whom he spoke to before and after services, he never spoke with Ms. Rodriguez. He nodded at her and offered his off-center smile, but he seemed like a shy schoolboy in her presence.

"Well, he's too old for her anyway," Mimi Jacquard judged in confidence to me one Sunday morning. "And for all we know, she's married."

"She has no wedding ring," I pointed out.

"Do Puerto Ricans wear them?" Mimi asked.

I replied that I was sure some married Latina women did not but that most would.

"Then she has a boyfriend," Mimi decided. "If Ernie's so interested, he would have found that out when he first knocked on her door."

"You think?" I said.

Mimi gave a little grunt. "He's too old for her."

That seemed true. He was old enough to be her father, if he had gotten started young. But that had not prevented him from inviting her to the calendar party.

One week before the event, I still had two tickets unsold. I had fixed my own wagon, complaining so much about the event that no one wanted to sit at the same table with a woman half crazed by its demands. I exhausted every person who ever owed me as much as a cup of coffee. In desperation and fully expecting his usual negative reply, I asked Ernie anyway. To my astonishment, he not only said yes but also bought both tickets. I never thought he would show, much less use the other ticket.

But Ernie arrived at St. Mark's with Lucia. For once, she had abandoned her formless dresses and wore a little black cocktail number, putting every other feminine figure in the building to shame. She also wore heels made out of ninety percent strap. Silver heels. The same rich, chestnut hair that we all knew in pigtails flowed around her face in soft waves. For Ernie's part, it turned out that one of the unseen closets in his house held an expensive, black, pin-striped suit and an elegant, silk regimental necktie.

People stayed two tables distant from my "Kickoff Month" table just so they could chatter about Lucia alone and Lucia with Ernie. Yet another reason why nobody dropped vote tickets into my fishbowl. But hot as the discussions got, Ernie and Lucia seemed more like father and daughter. They talked as much to those around them as to each other. They did not smile at each other with dating smiles. They never touched.

"Just a lonely, old bachelor using a neutral event to indulge his fantasies," I told myself. "And a kind, young woman using the same event to thank him for introducing her to her new church. No harm, no foul, no hits, no runs. No errors."

Except mine, of course.

CHAPTER NINE

IF YOU'RE LIKE me, you hate calculating the time of events when you read a story. I'll save you the trouble. Lucia Rodriguez first visited St. Mark's in early March. At that time she lived in her own apartment in Plainsboro and worked as a paralegal for a team of environmental lawyers. In spite of being intelligent, conservative, and cautious, the blindness of love had caused Lucia to fall for a handsome louse named Ricardo. The relationship was, like so many based on physical passion, a tumultuous one. When Ernie knocked on her door, he had used as one of St. Mark's inducements the very valuable, no-charge abilities of Jeremiah Hartmann at counseling.

Even pastors and psychiatrists need somebody to confide in from time to time. Jeremiah Hartmann uses me as a sounding board. This is, believe it or not, because when I'm told to keep something secret I can and do. I only set ink to paper now because this tale has reached its resolution, and someone must set the record straight and stop the ridiculous rumors and exaggerations. The other reason is that this cynical world needs to hear this tale.

In mid-April, the pastor told me that Lucia was receptive to his suggestions and that the relationship with Ricardo had reportedly improved. You may know that Will Shakespeare said something about "When sorrows come, they come not single spies but in battalions." So it was for Lucia. The last week of May, just before the calendar party, her employers announced that they were having too much trouble keeping the firm afloat and had both joined a larger firm in Trenton. The new firm did not need another paralegal, so she was out of work. Need I add that Lucia at the party with Ernie instead of Ricardo strongly suggested that she had not solved her first problem.

According to Pastor Hartmann, Lucia knew that she would be unable to keep her apartment on unemployment pay alone. Her contract lapsed on June 30th, but the landlord had a ready tenant and was willing to allow her to move out during the second week of June. Jeremiah made several suggestions, including a referral to Bernice Sherman, a member of St. Mark's who works at a local realty agency. He was quite amazed when I eventually confided to him her alternate solution to her residence problem.

If the neighbors of Skytop Road were curious about the moving van backed right to Ernie Love's garage when he moved in and the U-Haul he had used for the deer the previous December, they were like bloodhounds on the scent of fugitives from a chain gang when the little, yellow moving van paid a visit in mid-June. Several of the desperate phoned me immediately, convinced I would have the answer. Lucky for me, at the time I did not have to feign ignorance. It was only a few days later that I became enlightened. I happened to wake up after midnight to visit the bathroom. A sweep of headlights into our bedroom caused me to move to the windows. I was able to catch Lucia Rodriguez's blue Camry pull quickly into Ernie Love's second garage bay. I recognized the car from the church parking lot. I'm sure that even if a vigilant Neighborhood Watch warden like Dorothea Riley had seen what I saw, she would not know its significance. Lucia's car had never to my knowledge been on Skytop Road.

I returned to bed resolved to ignore what I had seen until absolutely compelled to acknowledge it. Nevertheless, it kept me up for another hour weighing all sorts of possibilities.

For the next seven days I never once saw the Camry out. Nor did Lucia emerge from the house. This was in late June. The New Jersey weather was, for a change, not too humid. Mother Nature beckoned. I spent almost as much time in the vegetable garden and flower beds as the rabbits. Ernie appeared briefly, but never enough for me to lasso him. I began to wonder with alarm if he had lost his pastoral position at the last church for abducting a young woman and keeping her prisoner in his basement.

And then Lucia Rodriguez made herself known on Skytop Road in the strangest way. She saved a life.

I already told you that my neighbor, Dorothea Riley, is a widow. Her husband died of a heart attack one month after retiring from his job at age sixty-five. I personally believed that once he saw what being at home with Dorothea 24/7 meant, the contemplation of limitless years of the same killed him. At any rate, she was alone. Her children were grown and living out of state. She never seemed to have visitors. She had a service tend to her lawn and garden. Other than her periodic automobile trips to various stores and her on-foot neighborhood fact-finding expeditions, one would have thought the house lights went on and off by timers.

Our newspaper delivery boy does not believe in driveways, sidewalks, or paths. His predawn route is a model of efficiency between houses. I know from walking Ralph the Wonder Mutt on snowy days that the lad cuts from one lawn to the next and hurls the papers from a distance at our front doors. Dorothea's entrance is masked by waist-high hedges. From ground level, no one near the street can tell if the newspaper has either been delivered or claimed. No one except a person who would be looking out the windows of the second front bedroom of Ernest Love's house.

Without a job and in no mood to face the world, Lucia Rodriguez was like Rapunzel in her bedroom tower. I previously related that Ernie had installed chic Levalor treatments on his windows. With the ability to adjust their openings infinitely, so long as she left her bedroom lights off Lucia could gaze out on her new surroundings without being seen. She had been warned by Ernie of Dorothea's spying and her binoculars, so she never came up directly to the blinds. She ventured close enough one morning, however, to see three newspapers on Dorothea's doorstep.

Concerned, Lucia crossed the street and rang the bell. No one answered. She rang again and put her ear to the door. She thought she heard a faint call. With more nerve than a spinal cord, she turned over close-by flowerpots, felt along ledges, checked under the doormat, and finally found a fake cast rock with a hollow center that held the front door key. She opened the door and called again. This time, Dorothea's pained voice was unmistakable.

Like the medical alert T.V. ads, Dorothea had fallen and couldn't get up. She had tripped on a corner of her coffee table and broken her hip. According to her, she had passed out for some hours. When she awoke, she tried to drag herself. The pile of the Berber rug had prevented her. She had lain helpless for more than two days.

The paramedics staffing the ambulance guessed that Dorothea would be in the hospital for perhaps a week, to have the hip fixed and to rebuild the old gal's strength. Hearing this, Lucia thoughtfully sought out the binoculars and tucked them into Dorothea's purse, so she could bring a little "home" with her. Then she cleaned the rug, washed the dishes in the sink, watered the plants, turned off the water, turned up the thermostat, locked the house, and hid the key.

That afternoon, Lucia went to the hospital to visit Dorothea, bringing roses from Ernie's garden. She visited two more times. The incident was what got Lucia out of hiding. The third time, she left her Camry out on the driveway. I was spreading dried blood where we had a tree removed the previous year. I crossed onto Ernie's property to say hello. In answer, Lucia raised a brown grocery bag.

"Can you come over in a few minutes for coffee?" I called out.

"I would like that," she said.

Over a couple of cups of French roast, I learned that Lucia and Ernie were "just good friends," that when he learned of her lost job he had offered one of his three spare bedrooms for free, and that Lucia was "using the opportunity to rearrange my life."

I let her say as much as she wanted and then showed a little of my feline side. "I'll bet Dorothea has been giving you the third degree, even when she was on morphine."

"I didn't give her the chance," Lucia replied. "The first time I visited, I volunteered that I had moved to Bunhouse 'from a distance.' She doesn't need to know from how far that is. I also said that Ernie is my friend, which he is, and that I'm storing my things and staying with him until I situate myself. I chattered about my work and my interests so fast that I'm sure she had trouble absorbing it all. I also asked her lots of questions about her and her life. She seemed to really enjoy that. Apparently, nobody in the neighborhood ever asks her about herself."

I realized with a guilty start that Lucia spoke the truth. Perhaps if her neighbors had shown some concern for her as a human being, Dorothea might have acted more like one than like a witch.

Lucia smiled broadly. "The second visit, when she asked personal questions, I said I told her already. She figures the accident affected her memory. She asked me very little of a personal nature today. I think she likes having me as a friend and is afraid of offending me. She thinks I'm Italian, but even that much ethnicity is too much for her, so she calls me Lucy." She took a sip of coffee and added, "She's being transferred to rehab at Merwick tomorrow. Maybe you could go with me to visit her in a few days." I told her that was a good idea.

We moved on to chat about St. Mark's and its members, the neighborhood, the best local stores. Before she left, I told Lucia that our lawyer had recently expressed the desire to find a competent part-time paralegal. I copied out his contact information from my private directory. Lucia expressed gratitude. However two weeks later, when I again talked to our lawyer about a writing contract, he said that he had not heard from her. I wondered just how radical Lucia's rearranging would be.

54

CHAPTER TEN

"OUT OF SIGHT, out of mind" really applied to Hubert Jasse that year, especially the part about being out of his mind. After his barrage of annoying but ineffectual dirty tricks against Ernie in January, February, and March, he took only half his usual proprietary walks around the neighborhood. He did not expend his energy gratuitously informing people how to improve their home exteriors or coaching them in the redesign of their gardens. He upgraded to a riding mower built for golf courses so he could be done all the sooner with his half acre of sod. There were no additions to his Easter or Memorial Day displays. It later became clear that he was spending hours brooding in his basement rec room about how to best Ernest Love, like Frankenstein contemplating his monster. It was the quiet before a demented brainstorm.

Hugh's unique brand of insanity used to be annually proven by his illegal Fourth of July fireworks party. Everyone in the neighborhood was invited for barbecued wings, beer on tap, margaritas, and mojitos. The party began at five in the afternoon, and by sundown – which of course is late in July – nobody who attended was feeling any pain. Neither did they feel any inhibitions about breaking the law. On the surface it seemed harmless enough, even ▾ generous, and Hugh was the first, the second, and the third one to tell you so. Having priced fireworks down at Chincoteague Island, I know that the stuff Hugh fired off had to cost collectively about a grand each year. We're talking the ones that zoom three hundred feet in the air and burst into multicolored pompoms with diameters a hundred feet wide. We're talking things that sit on the ground and create fountains and waterfalls of light, pinwheels of fire, and swords of flame. We're talking bombs that sound like the softening up of Iwo Jima before the landing assault.

Unfortunately, Hugh never bothered to learn how to properly handle such hazardous materials. In his drunken state, I don't think he ever cared. Proof of this was his churlish laughter every time he lit something. Since he used the street as his launching base, the real sky climbers could not be stuck into the asphalt. So Hugh stabbed them into a can filled with dirt. About every tenth time, either he stuck the explosive cockeyed in the can or else knocked the can over in his haste to escape before it went off. This resulted in flaming munitions screaming along parallel with the ground, bounding off little kids' strollers, damaging cars, exploding into landscaping, one year taking out the Stewarts' dining room window, and always terrorizing the dogs. It was rumored one of Hugh's errant rockets neutered a stray cat.

Naturally, the next morning the street was filthy with burn marks and the cardboard litter of spent fireworks. Hugh's philosophy was to let the next windstorm do his cleanup work.

This fateful year, as if to show that he merited the title Maestro of All Neighborhood Holiday Events, Hugh got his hands on pyrotechnics that only fire departments should handle. This class is not meant to be fired off anywhere but in huge open fields or on great expanses of water. Hundreds of elements fall back to earth still glowing. Which means they are on fire. Which means they can ignite larger fires.

In order to store his tons of holiday paraphernalia, Hugh had constructed in his backyard a shed with Amish barn proportions. The shed roof was made of wood shakes. I say "was" because the barn had to be replaced. One or more sparks came down on it that year still red hot and started a blaze that consumed twenty years of accumulated multi-holiday celebratory gimcracks and gewgaws. The plastic inflatables, the flags, the wooden cutouts, the wiring, the signs might as well have been tinder. I never saw anything go up so fast and burn so thoroughly. It was a three alarmer, producing in all six fire trucks (three of which my husband had sold) and nineteen firemen. If Hugh was looking to outdo himself that year, this was a tour de farce no one would ever try to top.

At first Hugh attempted to put out the flames with pitchers of leftover beer and mixed drinks, but of course the alcohol only added fuel to the fire. He got so winded from his frantic actions that all he could do after that was flop down on his patio, watch the holocaust, and weep. He wept even more when the police cited and Judge Cassato fined him for possessing fireworks and conducting a fireworks display without a license. He blubbered when the fire marshal cited and Judge Cassato fined him for constructing an impervious structure too close to his boundary line and with no building permit. He went on a full-day crying jag when his insurance company refused to replace an illegal shed and contents destroyed by illegal fireworks set off by the homeowner. Actually, what his agent told him was, "We don't insure stupidity. In fact, we'd rather you take your future business elsewhere…if you can find somebody who doesn't read the newspaper."

It was not merely the *Bunhouse Beacon* that made front-page material of Hugh's last fireworks party. A photojournalist who lives less than a mile from Skytop Road and who keeps his multi-band radio set to the police channel sold his story and pictures to both the *Times of Trenton* and the *Home News Tribune*. The coverage easily took up as much space as Hugh's Christmas wonders ever had.

Such public humiliation would subdue the average person. But cronies and family closed ranks around Hugh like he was the wounded patriarch water buffalo and the press was a pride of lions. They buoyed him up with the truth that perhaps a thousand people in the county had set off illegal fireworks that night and gotten away with it. They assured him that scores of homeowners erected sheds every year without permits and closer to the edge of their property than some rule-crazy zoning committee allowed. Best buddy Harry Covair even suggested that the extra big firework that burned down the shed had only been purchased because Hugh needed to make a statement to Ernest Love about the importance of celebrating holidays in the right spirit. The evening of the disaster, Harry had more spirits in him than any other two people at Hugh's party. Hugh adopted Harry's slurred statement as not only his official excuse but his rallying cry for a renewed Christmas spectacle.

I think everyone felt so badly for Hugh's catastrophic losses that they went overboard in their vocal support of "Good Will to Men." Blind to counterfeit sincerity, Hugh rallied with a vengeance. Three days after the fireworks fiasco, he illegally placed in every mailbox but Ernie's a flier announcing after a short preamble that [I duplicate this exactly] "The ashes of ill fate will provide the fertilizer for the most amazing Christmas holiday block display the county, the state, the nation, and perhaps the world has ever seen. The many expressions of effection and sympathy from wonderful neighbors like you has given me the courage not to merely rebuild a single homes decorative offering but to lead you all, like Moses leading the

Children of Isrial through the Red Sea to the Promised Land. Please attend the first planning session this Saturday at 3 Skytop Road. Beer and cocktails provided."

But badgering the neighborhood and planning the Christmas extravaganza was not enough to fill Hugh's agenda. There was the matter that Harry had shone a Bud light on. The disaster that Ernie had caused by his ungodly behavior had to be avenged.

CHAPTER ELEVEN

YOU KNOW HOW some mail you get has "Important Document; Do Not Destroy" or "Last Renewal Notice," emblazoned across its front, generally signifying that you can throw it away without opening it up? Colleges and universities should be required to print the warning "Unmitigated Nerve Inside" regarding their printed suggestions that parents of attending students build a new wing to the library or underwrite a new chair in Antarctic Architecture. This way, our heads may not explode from reading the message. I was standing at the mailbox, planning on returning the form with "You must have me confused with one of your alumni. I am already underwriting a Yale Drama major, thank you!" scribbled across it when Lucia came out of Dorothea's house. She was grinning.

"What's up?" I asked.

"Oh, I'm happy because Dotty is happy," she replied.

"Dotty, eh?"

"Yes. I'm Lucy, and she's Dotty."

"I always knew she was dotty," I said archly. "I thought I saw you two get out of her car about half an hour ago."

"Yes. She invited me in for coffee after we returned from the quilting circle."

"Are you interested in quilting?" I asked, thoroughly surprised.

Her grin got even wider. "Not at all. But I pretended to be because Dorothea once showed me a quilt her mother had made. And then I found a magazine on quilting near her television. So I told her I might be interested in quilting and knew of a group but that I was afraid to go alone. She was really happy to come with me."

"Betty at church belongs to a circle," I said.

"That's the one. I'll take Dotty a couple times and then tell her it's not my thing. By then she'll be hooked."

"I thought I was the queen of deviousness on this road," I

complimented her.

A whimsical expression altered Lucia's face. "You know, the old gal is an armchair philosopher. It must come from all those hours alone."

"What did she say?"

"She told me, 'I used to think that life is like an ice cream cone. Early on, you take little licks, testing it. Then you begin to bite huge chunks out of it, thinking it will last forever. But it doesn't. So at the end, you take smaller and smaller bites and licks, so you can savor every last bit. But by then it's just a few melted drops, and finally there's only a hollow cone that nobody wants.'"

"Wow!" I admired.

"But she wasn't finished. 'That was then,' she says to me, 'Now, I think life is like a rollercoaster. At first you enjoy the speed, the view, the climbs and drops. But after a while, you start thinking how dangerous it is. No matter how much you want to steer, the path is already made for you. You get sick to your stomach and bruised from the bumping, with painful hands from grabbing the safety rail, but it just keeps plunging and twisting. And the only way to get off before the end means killing yourself. So no matter what the ride throws at you, whether you're brave or not, you have to hang on. At the end, when it finally goes slower and slower and then stops, you're glad.'"

"Both pretty pessimistic perspectives," I said. "I think life is a great gift, with a greater gift afterward."

Lucia shrugged. "I think life is like taking public transportation, but you both have your points."

I laughed as I studied her face and then her stomach. Her face was fuller and rosier than when I had first met her. Under her formless shift, I thought I saw a bit of a belly. I wondered if a single lady unused to regular meals was being fine wined and fatted calf dined by Ernie Love. When I looked up, she had started to blush.

"Oh, I was just about to say you not only look happy but healthy," I hastened to declare. Lucia recovered and dipped her head slightly. "Thank you."

I added, "I was going to ask you to come with me to the Lenahans this afternoon, but you're probably"

"The Lenahans from St. Mark's?"

"Yes. You don't know about Tom and Mary?"

"No. What?"

"Have you given the church your e-mail or phone?"

She winced. "I did when I first joined, but they've both changed."

A great deal had happened since Lucia had attended church on Sunday. Another driver had lost control of his car and struck Tom Lenahan straight on. The air bag had deployed, but bones had broken in both his lower legs. Thanks to something called DRGs, Princeton Medical Center had to discharge him to a traction bed in his home after only four days. His wife, Mary, had been so upset following the accident that she had consumed virtually nothing but vending machine peanuts while at the hospital. After her violent stomach pains continued for several days, she, too, had been admitted to the hospital. The diagnosis was acute diverticulitis. She and Tom were returning as invalids to their home and two children, who were both under ten.

I had volunteered to coordinate the support team for the Lenahans. I estimated that Mary would be all right to handle her family obligations within a week. Until then, the children had to be supervised, fed, helped with homework, driven to private lessons, gotten on the bus. All meals had to be provided for. Grocery shopping and laundry had to be done. The house needed to be kept straight. After Mary recovered, the lawn still needed watering and mowing, and errands around town had to be run so she could stay with her husband. Later Tom would have to be driven for follow-ups and physical therapy. I had developed daily task charts and penciled in volunteers by their particular strengths.

More than forty church members volunteered to help. I have observed in my fifty years on this earth that only a small percentage of humanity are seriously damaged by nature and/or nurture. These are the ones who cause ninety percent of society's woes. Perhaps another ten percent consistently run red lights, steal if temptation is placed before them, indulge in bad habits that cause them to make bad decisions, and the like. Given the right circumstances or enough prodding, it is possible to move these folk to altruistic acts. But the vast majority of people are instinctively and generously good. All they need to hear is that their gifts are needed, and they step forward. One reason I have always been a member of a church family is that the statistics there run to more than ninety percent good. I wanted Lucia to come with me not only because I knew she is a naturally giving person but also because I wanted her to be able to witness to

Ernie how beneficial it can be to have a support family built around God and His love.

We arrived at the Lenahan house to find Mary at the front door and two men from a surgical supply company delivering a traction bed for Tom. They set the bed up in the living room. When they left, Lucia set to rearranging the room to make it easier to use. Meanwhile, I consulted with Mary on the schedules I had sketched out, modifying them to her desires. When she excused herself to go to the bathroom, I went to Lucia. She stood with her arms folded, studying the living room.

"This will work much better if we temporarily put the sofa over there," she decided.

I pushed up my sleeves. "I agree. You grab one end and I'll lift the other."

"I can't," she said softly. "I'm pregnant."

CHAPTER TWELVE

AS ERNIE LOVE once said through his sagely smile, "What goes 'round comes 'round."

We now arrive at the August following the Great Fireworks Conflagration. We take you once again to the Bunhouse Municipal Court. It looks exactly like the court in the movie version of *To Kill a Mockingbird.* Except that it's a lot smaller. And there's no balcony. And there are no Black people or children present. And Gregory Peck's missing, too. Other than that, you get the picture.

At the defendant's desk, where Dr. Ernest Love had sat in January, sits Hugh Jasse. The symmetry of the situation makes my toadstool heart jump for perverted joy. The irony increases when Ernie arrives only a minute before the proceedings begin and plops himself down right next to Harry Covair and Joe Ciaro, exactly where Hugh had sat.

As a journalist, I hate interrupting interviews to jot down notes. Instead, I produce a highly sensitive pocket recorder and ask if I may use it. This same recorder sits unobtrusively on my lap during the court session. Therefore, you may be assured that the following dialogue is word for word. The visual observations, however, are mine, all mine.

Judge Dominick Cassato enters, not looking happy at wearing a suit on a sweltering August afternoon. The air conditioning is incapable of cooling a courtroom packed to the walls. He takes his seat on the bench.

The bailiff calls the court in session and then summons the Maestro of All Neighborhood Holiday Events to the podium directly across from the judge.

"Mr. Jasse," Dominick Cassato says in a less-than-cheerful voice.

"Good afternoon, Your Honor."

"We should be charging you rent, you're here so often."

Cassato opens a folder and, without consulting it, says, "We are here today in the question of the willful destruction of private property."

"I would like to protest, Your Honor," Hugh chirps.

"Please give me the opportunity to ask first how you plead."

"Not that, sir." He filled his lungs to deliver his rehearsed speech. "Since you were the judge the previous times I was here, and since you fined me a great deal of money for that business with my shed and   basically decided in Mr. Love's favor the time before, shouldn't you excuse yourself?"

Cassato's head rears back ever so slightly from the suggestion. "The word you are grasping for is 'recuse,' Mr. Jasse. It means that a judge or jury is self-interested in a case, is prejudiced, or is incompetent to decide the case. None of these holds true here. This trial will proceed. Do you have counsel?"

"I'm serving as my own lawyer."

"Perfect. The charge compasses the spreading of salt on the front of lawn at 18 Skytop Road. Further, that the pattern in which the salt was spread spelled out 'Atheist' when the grass died. You, Mr. Jasse, are accused as the perpetrator of this malicious and destructive act. How do you plead?"

"Not guilty, Your Honor. Ernie Love has it in for me."

"A simple 'not guilty' will suffice," Cassato says. "How do you feel about atheists, Mr. Jasse?"

Hugh shrugs. "It doesn't matter how I feel. God will get them all in the end."

"Question answered. Are you a religious man?"

"Sure. I'm Catholic."

"Do you belong to a church?"

"I belong to St. Jude, right here in Bunhouse."

"I belong to St. Jude," Cassato says, as if correcting him. "I have never seen you there."

I wish at this moment that I had put myself nearer to the defendant's desk, so I could watch the expression of fear forming.

"I go on Christmas and Easter. It's crowded then. That must be the reason."

"Let's not prolong this any more than we have to," Cassato says.

At that moment, a cell phone rings.

"All cell phones were to be turned off before proceedings began," the judge reminds in an annoyed voice. "Whose is that?"

Hugh winces as he digs into his pocket and produces the offending phone. He flips it up to turn it off.

"Ah-ah-ah!" Cassato warns. His waggling hand with raised forefinger turns palm side up and extends, demanding the phone from our defendant. Hugh rises and sets the phone in Cassato's hand.

The judge presses the TALK button.

"Hello?" His eyebrows knit for a moment, and then he gives Hugh a hard, unblinking look. He listens in silence for several seconds. He clears his throat, takes the phone from his ear, and studies the message panel. He looks once more at Hugh, and I know the cat is about to eat the canary. "Your caller I.D. has identified a fellow named Bobbie B. What a modern world we live in! Bookies, like doctors and dentists, are now using automated messages."

This causes a verbal commotion in the courtroom, one that the judge does not quell. He is busy scrolling through Hugh's phone list to find the number associated with Bobbie B. He snatches up a pencil and pulls a tablet of paper in front of him and copies the number down.

"It seems that you owe Bobbie B. six hundred dollars, that payment is overdue, and that he is notifying you that he is billing your MasterCard." Judge Cassato smirks. "I hope you at least get air miles." He looks at the Chief of Police, who is sitting in the front row. He holds up the pad. The chief takes it and disappears up the aisle and out the courtroom double doors.

The judge sets the cell phone down. "Back to the matter at hand." Cassato looks at Ernie. "Dr. Love, would you please take the plaintiff seat?"

"Certainly, Your Honor."

"I understand from your complaint that since shortly after you appeared in this courtroom concerning your display of dead deer, that you have been pestered by realtors, chimneysweeps and the like, all of whom received calls from someone claiming to be you and requesting service."

"That's correct."

"Dog feces were also left in your mailbox. The flowers from your garden removed. Your satellite television dish antenna's wires were cut on the night prior to the Super Bowl?"

The collective gasp at this last news lowered the room air pressure several points. There are depths beyond bottom, and preventing a red-blooded American man from viewing the Super

Bowl is one of them.

"Also true," Ernie affirmed.

"Were you able on any of those occasions to ascertain without a reasonable doubt the person or persons harassing you?"

"I was not."

I turn to study Joe Ciaro and Harry Covair. Their returning expressions are those of choirboys. And we all know how innocent choirboys are.

The judge sucks in his cheeks briefly and makes a perplexed noise. "Likewise, with the spreading of salt on your lawn, you are unable to fix blame."

"No, Your Honor. This time I have proof. However, I need a monitor and a CD player connected to it."

Cassato grins. "No problem. We have those in the building."

More witness noise. It's like being on the set of Perry Mason.

As if cued by a stage manager in the wings, the Chief of Police returns through the double doors carrying the aforementioned monitor and small CD player. In rapid order they are plugged into an outlet and positioned on a rostrum so that the entire courtroom can see. Ernie takes from his attaché case a jewel box, opens it, removes a CD, and pops it into the player.

"The mischief to my property always took place between midnight and dawn," Ernie explains. "So I set up four miniature cameras, all well hidden, to cover my front and back yards. Here are the images captured on July 19th of this year, as you will see from the automatic dating system appearing at the bottom right side of the screen."

Ernie fast forwards to 3:14 A.M. The system displays to us a different camera view every ten seconds. Each time it comes to the front lawn, it captures an image of Hubert Jasse holding a bag of rock salt and carefully spilling it out in a pattern.

"Can you freeze that right there? Remarkable clarity, Dr. Love," Judge Cassato observes, in an upbeat voice. "I have a beach house that needs surveillance. Is this technology available to the public?"

"Actually not yet, Your Honor," Ernie answers, matching the judge's breezy tone of voice. "This was developed by NASA. But you know how technology is. If there's a buck to be made, it will be on store shelves soon enough. No, this is a hypersensitive infrared reader that translates to a picture easily seen by the human eye."

Cassato tents his hands and rests his chin on his knuckles, apparently engrossed in analyzing Hugh's *in flagrante delicto* performance. "Very easily indeed. Let it roll again, please. I can even make out that mole just in front of Mr. Jasse's left ear."

"I would like to change my plea, Your Honor," Hugh chokes out.

"I'll bet you would. You can turn off the machines now, Dr. Love."

"But I wasn't under oath yet," Hugh points out.

"I see. Your habit is to lie until you're under oath, is it?" Suddenly, Cassato's affable expression hardens like quick-drying cement. He sits up very straight. "This is about as open-and-shut a case as I have ever tried. So let my judgment be as swift. Dr. Love, what was the cost of removing the lawn and affected underlying soil, replacing the soil, and sodding the lawn?"

Ernie produces photocopies of receipts.

The judge scans the documents. "This seems very reasonable."

"I did the work myself," Ernie reveals.

"And we must not forget the significant cost of watering this time of year."

I see Hugh's shoulders relax. He believes he is about to get away solely with financial restitution. He is too dense to see that he has been cast in a cautionary tale as the arch villain, and not nearly enough punishment has been meted out to satisfy the crime.

Again, Dominick Cassato turns his stern countenance on the defendant. "I understand that you consider yourself a leader in your local community."

"I guess so," Hugh agrees in a small voice, perhaps beginning to realize how well he has been set up.

"Shame on you then! Childish, malicious harassment is not the act of a leader. You will pay to Dr. Love the cost of his replacement soil and sod and another hundred dollars for water. Don't sigh with relief quite yet, Mr. Jasse. As with the business of Dr. Love's punishment last year, I see no point in wasting the taxpayer's hard-earned money on jail time."

"I'll do fifty hours of service at St. Jude," Hugh volunteers with haste.

"I'm fairly sure St Jude won't want you. No, I have seen photographs of your abilities with holiday decoration. I understand you have had an idea to raise money for charity, using your outdoor decorating skills and those of others on your street."

Now Hugh sits ramrod straight. "I do indeed, Your Honor," he says with relish.

Cassato's hand goes up. "However...what you have presented in the past has nothing to with the true message of the season. I am convinced this is what Dr. Love protested on two consecutive years, touching off this ridiculous squabble. I need someone who claims more traditional tastes to guide the theme. I choose you, Dr. Love."

Ernie blinks a couple times. "What?"

"And your home, Dr. Love, will display part of the overall production."

Harry Covair brays in protest. "What the hell does he know about outdoor illumination?"

"Another such outburst and you will be held in contempt of court," Cassato warns. He turns again to Ernie. "You have stated in this court your loss of faith. That is no excuse for avoiding this task. The display need not be overtly religious. My primary desire is something that inspires people of our community to be better neighbors to each other. Furthermore, I want you two to work together. I believe that familiarity breeds understanding and not contempt. This matter is closed, pending satisfaction of my judgments. If my instructions are not carried out, however, there will be jail time served."

Now, I fully expected Ernie to protest. But he did not. For a moment, I thought that he and the judge had cooked up not merely the little drama about the camera images together. Looking into Ernie's astonished face the moment after Cassato appointed him designer of the holiday spectacular, however, changed my mind. As I shut off my recorder, I began to formulate the theory that Judge Cassato, devout Catholic that he was, hoped to coax a lost sheep back into the fold. In my fertile mind I saw him consulting with Pastor Hartmann as to Ernie's fulfillment of his community service at St. Mark's, hearing that Ernie seemed more interested in God than he cared to admit, and hatching his salvation plot.

I started to ponder why Ernie had not put up more of a fight against serving as the design chairman for the Skytop Road winter show, but another mystery dominated my thoughts. How, I asked myself, would a man with a Doctor of Divinity degree know about the latest infrared detection technology from the National Aeronautics and Space Administration, and, even more amazingly, how could he get his hands on the equipment?

70

CHAPTER THIRTEEN

I TAILED ERNIE Love one last time, lying in wait for him in a parking space at the top of Princeton's Alexander Road. I got the definitive answer I sought about his profession, and I promise to share the truth with you. But, as I have said, I can keep a secret. I kept it then, and I'm keeping it now. You will just have to wait until the end of the tale.

In the weeks following the second trial, Hubert Jasse's public approval rating slipped lower than Hitler's as the Russians entered Berlin. The stringer photojournalist who had covered the fireworks barn burning had evidently researched all the back elements of the Skytop Road Christmas display feud and turned it, along with the latest trial, into a full-page newspaper cause célèbre in Central Jersey. The residents did not take kindly to Hugh making our neighborhood into a laughingstock, including a drive-time hour of sarcastic discussion and call-ins to Jersey 101.5 radio. The new meeting called by Hugh regarding a concerted Skytop holiday display did not rouse RSVPs from even his henchmen. I was compelled to step in and act as the voice of reason. I formulated a letter concentrating on the need to resolve the debacle publicly so we could all regain our pride. The letter also reminded everyone that a worthy charity was now expecting to benefit from our efforts. I mailed the letters out and followed up with phone calls, and more or less the entire street met at my house just before Labor Day. In the end, everyone went away feeling better and, I might say with personal pride, enthused. We were, after all, in the spotlight for our fifteen minutes of fame, and it was up to us to determine how our story ended.

What is more, everything is relative. What seemed like a scandal before the meeting shrank to minuscule proportions when everyone saw that the woman living at Ernest Love's house had no wedding ring but was more than a little pregnant. The shock turned to profound confusion when Dorothea Riley showed for the meeting, all smiles, sat beside Lucia, and held her hand like a long-lost daughter.

"Welcome to Wonderland," my husband whispered to me.

Meantime, at good old St. Mark's tongues were wagging faster than a kennel club show on a dog day afternoon. Lucia continued to sit in her accustomed seat, and Ernie sat behind her. Not a soul asked Lucia Rodriquez about the growing bulge in her midsection. Then again, nary a soul spoke to her. But they talked plenty away from her.

Lucia had not yet declared that she wished membership in St. Mark's. She was officially a constant visitor. This put the disapprovers in a quandary as to what they could or should say. It's tough to shun somebody who's not a member of the community. Nevertheless, there was no doubt that at least some members of the congregation intended to speak out at the semi-annual congregational meeting just after Labor Day. Morton Finch, John Whitworth, and Augusta Rettig, all loud talkers, would temporarily overcome their patent antipathies toward each other to form an unholy alliance. Augusta had clearly signaled her attitude by moving her seat to the right side of the church. This tectonic upheaval had a domino effect, rearranging the human furniture so much that the place was barely recognizable. There is little as sacrosanct in a church or synagogue as the seating protocol.

From his everyday bearing and even when he engages in casual, non-church conversation, Pastor Jeremiah Hartmann seems like just a regular guy. Perhaps he is. Perhaps he becomes a genius whenever the Holy Spirit chooses to sit upon his shoulder. Whatever the case, he had the answer to quell the brewing crisis.

On the Sunday of the year's second congregational meeting almost everyone comes to the earlier service, packing the seats. Pastor Hartmann took his opportunity and ran with it during the sermon. I never checked the calendar of church readings to see if he had purposely substituted the Gospel reading that day or if Providence had placed the right one where needed. Jeremiah always types out his sermons verbatim. He allows those of us who stay awake enough to be impressed by his wisdom to have copies. Here are the highlights.

"Oh Lord, let all with ears hear and all with eyes see. Amen. Today's Gospel bears repeating. 'Early in the morning he came again to the temple; all the people came to him, and he sat down and taught them. The scribes and the Pharisees brought a woman who had been caught in adultery, and placing her in the midst, they said to him, "Teacher, this woman has been caught in the act of adultery. Now in the law Moses commanded us to stone such. What do you say about her?" This they said to test him, that they might have some charge to bring against him. Jesus bent down and wrote with his finger on the ground. And as they continued to ask him, he stood up and said to them, "Let him who is without sin among you be the first to throw a stone at her." And once more he bent down and wrote with his finger on the ground.'

"We have been talking off and on this year, my Christian friends, about the prayer Jesus gave us to say. You know…the one that starts, 'Our Father'? Today's passage from John touches upon 'Forgive us our sins, as we forgive those who sin against us.' What exactly does the word 'as' mean? Might it mean 'in direct proportion to how we forgive those who sin against us'? Well, that would set most of us in bad standing, wouldn't it? Imagine only having each of our sins forgiven when we forgive one of somebody else!

"Back in 1988, Robert Fulghum wrote the wildly successful *All I Really Needed to Know I Learned in Kindergarten*. It's filled with wonderful maxims such as 'Let Others Play with Your Toys' and 'Always Take a Nap.' The kindergarten maxim that applies to this sermon is 'Worry About Yourself.' Take the log out of your own eye to be able to see clearly the mote in the other guy's eye.

"We're always watching others and judging, aren't we? It reminds me of the old Jewish joke about the woman who throws a party. She walks up to a guest and says, 'Have an egg roll?' The guest answers, 'No, thanks. I've already had two.' 'You've had four,' the hostess replies, 'but who's counting?'"

"But is this really our fault? I mean God made our eyes and ears facing outward. It's hard to look at and hear ourselves. Maybe that's why the Bible has to tell us so often to love our neighbors. Leviticus tells us in Chapter 19 that 'You shall love thy neighbor as thyself.' Solomon tells us that it is the godless man who destroys his neighbor with his mouth. Proverbs also warns us not to 'plan evil against your neighbor who dwells trustingly beside you.' And this is the vengeful Old Testament. You all know that the New Testament exhorts us to love our neighbors in practically every book.

"'But,' you say, 'what about when my neighbor commits a sin to society?' Then the question begged is: Who's to say what a sin is? Sins change with time and societies, don't they? Our country fought the bloodiest war on this soil over the question of keeping slaves. For thousands of years slavery wasn't a sin. It's in the Bible. The ancient Greek philosophers, those great debaters over the meaning of goodness and justice, did not deplore the practice.

"What about bigamy? In Solomon's time, men were allowed many wives. Now, you can't even get away with it in Utah.

"Back in the time of Jesus, if a man was betrothed to a woman and she became pregnant, nobody gave it another thought. Happened all the time. Nowhere are Joseph or Mary taken to task for Mary being pregnant but not yet his wife. In fact, her baby got presents from kings.

"Today, we're entertained by soap operas that celebrate infidelity on a daily basis. State after state only acknowledges adultery as a sin when it is contributory to divorce. And yet, in Jesus's day, women were stoned for adultery.

"Why did Jesus write in the dirt? The most common opinion among Biblical scholars is that he knew the dark sins of those who hoped to trap Jesus with the law of Moses. He wrote down their sins as a threat to expose them. It worked, and the woman lived. We do not know if this adulterous woman mended her ways, but I like to think after such a demonstration of love and forgiveness, and by the grace and power of the Holy Spirit, she sinned no more in that manner.

"My Christian friends, when it comes to you and me judging individuals we must be like the person who tempers his temper by counting to ten. Ask yourself before you judge: Is this indeed a sin? If so, is it mine to judge? Rather, is there something positive I can do for the sinner to help her or him sin no more instead of judging and demanding change? Have I made my own life pure enough to be a shining light, a clear example to impress sinners to change their way?

"'Worry about yourself.' Do not cast stones unless you are blameless. 'Judge not lest thou be judged.' 'Love thy neighbor as thyself.' 'Let all with ears hear and all with eyes see. Amen.'"

Let me tell you, the ears were opened that morning. But the mouths were not. It was obvious that speaking no evil did not mean that evil wasn't being thought. During the ensuing meeting, no one sat near Lucia. Afterward, when the narthex was filled, a visible circle existed around her as if she carried the Black Death.

At almost the exact time I discovered the secret of Ernie

Love's profession, I also learned the story behind Lucia's pregnancy. But being the perverse creature I am, I kept silence. I wanted all those who spoke and thought the worst eventually to regret not worrying about themselves.

What Pastor Hartmann's sermon did not quell at the congregational meeting was the discussion about scholarships.

"I see nothing in the report about the college scholarship funds," Henrietta Fowler observed, after the minutes of the last meeting had been approved.

"What scholarship fund?" our church president replied.

"What do you mean 'what scholarship?'" Henrietta said with a tinge of attitude.

Rich held up his hands. "Okay, before we begin sounding like Abbott and Costello, tell me what you've heard."

"As I understand it, the child of any member of this congregation who qualifies as far as low family income and high academic standing can receive a scholarship that will pay full tuition to Mercer County Community College for both years."

This was clearly news to the congregation, and instantly they set out among themselves trying to get at the truth without lifting their posteriors from the pews. Rich called for quiet for a full fifteen seconds.

"Who told you this, Mrs. Fowler?" Rich asked.

Henrietta swung around and stared at Ernie. "Mr. Love did when he first visited my home."

I think Moses would have created less commotion if he had walked into the sanctuary at that moment.

"Are you aware that Mr. Love is not a member of this church?" Rich asked Henrietta.

"Say what?"

Rich extended his hand toward Ernie. "The floor is all yours, sir."

Ernie stood. "It is true that I am not a declared member of St. Mark's. However, I have established at the Princeton Bank and Trust a sizable account that is solely earmarked for college scholarships. This is available to the children of members of this congregation."

An auditory version of "The Wave" passed from the front pew to the back.

"Were you aware of this fund, Pastor?" Rich asked.

Pastor Hartmann stood. "Dr. Love had mentioned it to me some months ago, but I thought it prudent not to make it public unless and until he had become a member. I had no idea he had used his fund as an enticement to increase membership."

"Yes! That's exactly what he did!" Morty cried out, standing. "He went into Ashton like the Pied Piper and brought families here under false pretenses. He did it purely to stir up trouble, because he hates churches and God!"

"For once will you hold your tongue, you old idiot?" Leonard Carrington demanded.

"Make me!" Morty shot back.

The slamming of a hymnal brought surprised silence.

You haven't heard me say much about my husband, William Robert Morn. He is generally a man of few words. That's why our marriage has lasted so long. But when William speaks, people listen. He had served a three-year term as church president in the not-so-distant past.

"Do we forget that we are in God's house?" he asked in a chastening voice. "Maybe it's good that we let all the pent-up venom spit out, but not in this place. We now have people of color in our church. A number of us were raised in houses and schools that reeked of prejudice. This may as easily be Black prejudice toward what it means to be White. But Dr. Love forced us to confront that. Maybe he even tricked us into it. Let's say for the moment that he is an atheist with the worst intentions. Did he succeed? Or are we a better church and a better Christian family now, whatever his intentions? Are we not more financially secure? Will we be here in five years...as Dr. Love asked us at the last meeting?" He turned to Ernie. "Make your statement and your promise to this church concerning these scholarships, please."

Ernie cleared his throat. "I have put aside enough money in a restricted account to enable every child in this church to attend two years of community college. Providing he or she graduates with a B average, and providing he or she maintains that average at the college, the money is available. Tomorrow, I will produce a signed and witnessed document to that effect, along with a copy of the account statement."

"Why would you do this, Dr. Love?" Mimi Jacquard asked.

"That's my own business, Ms. Jacquard," he replied.

I knew about Ernie's profession, I knew about Lucia's baby,

and I knew about why Ernie had funded the scholarships. But the answers were not mine to give.

78

CHAPTER FOURTEEN

PLANNING A TRULY impressive, coordinated neighborhood Christmas display is a great deal of work. To keep the peace and see that all my efforts to this point did not break down, I volunteered to serve as arbitrator between Ernie and Hugh. After much wrangling, they settled on basically the same story we told in St. Mark's Living Nativity. The idea was not to proselytize Christianity overtly but at least to tell the story of the birth that inspired the holiday…or Holy Day, as Ernie insisted on calling it. From the time I had seen his "Xmas Is Cancelled" display and realized it was a reaction to Hugh and Crew, I knew that only a man with deep religious convictions would be offended enough to go to such lengths. If his faith was in turmoil, something truly horrific had to have happened to leave him dangling between heaven and hell.

The banner stretched over the bottom of Skytop Road would read "Hope Made Visible." The banner at the opposite end would read "Peace on Earth. Good Will Toward Men." Unlike St. Mark's Living Nativity, there would be no readings from the Gospels. If a viewer was an adult Christian, the story was well known. If a child was curious about the meaning of each tableau, an adult in the car could choose to tell the child whatever he or she felt appropriate. If a non-believer wanted to view the road purely as an impressive, beautiful display, so be it.

Hugh insisted that "If we're gonna do it, we have to do it up right." There were to be no Homosote or plywood cut-out people. Ernie countered that there was no way we could get real people to stand outside from dark until midnight for an entire pre-Christmas week, no matter how dedicated they were. The cold weather and other obligations made that impossible. We seemed at an impasse until everyone came together for the street meeting. Joyce Ann Ricciardi is a store manager at the local Macy's. She knew that they were getting rid of sixteen shopworn mannequins. She suggested that we clothe and pose those figures for the most important scenes and use them as "extras" whenever real actors volunteered. Unlike Hugh, Joan Mitchell was a frequent worshiper at St. Jude. She knew that the choir had just gotten new robes and that the old, ecru-colored ones would serve well as shepherd costumes. Lucia and Dorothea volunteered to make specific costumes as required.

These suggestions gave me a bold idea. For years, I had been discontent with merely showing our Living Nativity, "the county's most inspiring Christmas presentation," on the grassy lot beside our church. The venue threatened many non-members who rightly supposed they would be corralled during the post-performance hot cocoa and cookies and given a pitch for prospective membership. Taking our show literally on the road, however, would witness to thousands. A sign at the bottom of the street would acknowledge St. Mark's and its members. Newspaper coverage would be huge. We merely needed to relocate. It wasn't exactly going into all the world, but it was a start.

I presented the notion to the church counsel and our nativity director, George Reeder. They loved the idea. Suddenly, the Skytop Road extravaganza had a Herod's palace, a fake stone wall for sheep, a stable and manger made out of old barn wood, twenty good costumes, two full-sized fake sheep with real wool covering, shepherd's crooks, treasure chests, wiring, lights, and music.

Somehow, the Illumination Mafia understood the plan. Hugh's house would actually be dark for the first time in two decades. Only his front lawn would hold a spotlighted scene of the three Wise Men following the Star. Hugh, Harry, and Joe all volunteered many hours to serve as the kings, and mannequins were available for the other hours. Incredibly, each of them sprang for a full-sized, realistic beast of burden. Hugh negotiated with one of the Mummer string bands in Philly for a giant fake camel with a saddle; Harry rustled up a plaster horse left over from a mall display; and Joe found a stuffed jackass at a famous Lambertville flea market. I held my tongue when Joe started telling neighbors that the creature was Hugh's second cousin.

The Rothman household also surprised me. Irv was not a practicing Jew, but neither had he jettisoned his heritage. His attitude was "You're all worshiping a Jew. How opposed to this should I be?" In order to remind onlookers that this story sprang from the Rod of Jesse, he created an impressive, three-dimensional synagogue with menorahs burning in the windows. He also provided in his backyard a Star of David hoisted high on a barren tree, so that Hugh, Harry,and Joe had something to point to.

Those who traveled Skytop Road would see several properties decorated, as a distant towns, as a Roman guard post, as the shops of Bethlehem and the fields where shepherds watched their flocks by night. At 12 Skytop, Mike Taylor would fix a dozen dolls done up as angels to the ridge of his roof, along with speakers piping out angelic music.

The Morn property was chosen as the strategic place to put the stable and manger. It made sense. So many of the actors were friends from church that it was less imposition for me to open my front and garage doors to them to change costumes, wet their whistles, drain their bladders, and get warm periodically from the cold.

As the weeks passed, neighbors became more and more involved in the planning and execution, suggesting improvements and volunteering to create them. Several banded together to form a publicity committee. The teenagers painted signs and planned the money collection.

Other than approving changes, Ernie and Lucia were largely left out. His place was to be one of the dark, interim properties needed to separate the scenes. Underneath all the excitement and camaraderie of the Skytop Spectacular, the stigma of an unmarried and pregnant woman living with a man old enough to be her father made the neighbors uneasy. Naturally, people knew that I was friendly with both of them, so nothing negative was said to me. But the silence on the subject was deafening.

Hugh and Ernie had finally come to terms with each other. On Skytop Road, all was calm, all would soon be bright. But all was still not right.

CHAPTER FIFTEEN

THE FRIDAY BEFORE Christmas, Jeremiah Hartmann came down with strep throat. By Saturday morning, he had completely lost his voice. Do you have any idea how difficult it is finding a replacement preacher for the Sunday before Christmas on twenty hours' notice? Let me tell you: It's nigh unto impossible. Those who are not glued to their own parish are augmenting other churches or traveling. At least in Central New Jersey they are.

We have plenty of veteran worship assistants who can conduct services from memory. Our religion does not require a degreed minister to lead the worship. The administration of the sacraments can be eliminated for the week. But the sermon is a different matter.

I was doing last-minute work with a couple other ladies of the church on the Skytop Spectacular costumes when Rich Parker walked in.

"Well, I found somebody to deliver the sermon."

"Who?" I asked.

"Your next-door neighbor."

"Ernie?"

"The same."

"You must be kidding!"

"I am not. Somehow, he heard about Jeremiah's strep and volunteered."

"After all the surprises he's pulled on this church, are you crazy enough to let him?" Lynette Novak asked.

"I called Jeremiah. Mrs. Pastor spoke for him and said that he not only will allow Ernie to speak but encourages him to."

"Isn't Ernie rather busy," I checked in, "considering the stork dropped a baby at his house four days ago?"

Rich flung his hands wide. "You would know more about that than I would."

In that he spoke the truth. I, being a member of the Inner Circle at the Love house, had spent many hours there of late. I had confided to Ernie in early December that I knew his secrets, had known them for months, and had told no one. Moments later, I was inside the domicile so many neighbors longed to view. It was well furnished, with a woman's touch. I was informed that the woman was not Lucia.

Lucia had given birth to a boy. He was healthy and beautiful, with a baby version of Latino features. As of Saturday, Lucia still had not divulged his real name. I called him "Bundle," which was short for bundle of joy. Dorothea, the only other person on our road allowed in, called him "Angel," short for Christmas angel. When Lucia picked up the nickname, Dotty bristled. "Like hell you'll call him On-hell!"

"But it's the correct Spanish pronunciation," Lucia protested.

"Then call him 'Bundle'."

Inside the church office, I helped Rich lower his protesting hands. "Lucia has enough help, I think."

Our belabored church president sighed. "Man, I was hoping for a quiet Christmas. Tell him to do me a personal favor and not make any waves. Please!"

I promised I would.

Just before dark that Saturday night, an hour before the well-publicized Skytop Road Holiday Spectacular was officially lit, Ernie knocked on my door.

"I want an incredibly big favor from you," he said.

I shoved Ralph the Wonder Mutt gently away from Ernie's crotch. "Name it."

"I need to move the stable and manager over to my house. I forgot that Judge Cassato said I had to have part of the display on my property. He's going to be here tonight!"

"Are you kidding?" I barked. "Do you know how much work—"

"Hugh, Harry, and Joe are waiting outside. The four of us can move it and change the lighting in thirty minutes, tops."

I could see that this meant a great deal to Ernie. I also liked the sound of him and the Illumination Mafia working together under extreme conditions.

"Hey, go ahead," I allowed. "We'll just have to march the

actors another hundred feet."

"Speaking of that, I'd like another favor, but I'll ask you tomorrow morning, in church."

The stable and manger were moved in record time. I was not needed as the Innkeeper's Wife for the first time in years, so William and I trudged down the road to see what was going on.

Anticipating a crowd, the Bunhouse police had erected barricades and flow lanes through the neighborhood. Cars were backed up as far as the eye could see. Liam and his buddies stood ready with their Mason jars to collect contributions for the Goodwill Society. Music was already playing. There was not an inflatable decoration in sight. The air was cold, but there was no sign of snow, which I lamented aloud. Then William pointed out that there was no mention of snow in the Bible. When he began lecturing about Christmas originally being a pagan holiday appropriated by the Romans to attract more believers and that Jesus was probably born in the spring, when the census was more likely, I clapped my hand over his mouth and told him to just look and enjoy.

Opening night was a triumph. Hugh had coordinated and constructed to a fare-thee-well. The players were pumped. The lights were splendid. Even Hugh's hogging of the television coverage did not dampen the event. We all looked forward to several more nights of outdoor theater with a real Holy Day spirit.

86

CHAPTER SIXTEEN

NORMALLY, THE ADVENT Sunday before Christmas garners a good attendance. It's not the two services on Christmas Eve, mind you, but it's impressive. For this Sunday, the choir always sings both services. I was, therefore, sitting in the front row of the loft when Dr. Ernest Love walked to the pulpit with no sermon in his hand.

Ernie looked out at the sea of fresh-scrubbed faces and red clothing. He cleared his throat. For a moment, his face scrunched up.

"I see a few faces I don't know, but most of you know me. My name is Ernie Love. I wasn't always Ernie Love. Most of my life, I was Ernst Lieb. It sounds foreign. That's because both my parents came to this country from Germany. They settled in Missouri. That's where I grew up."

Ernie smiled his crooked smile. "I've been rather secretive about my life since moving to New Jersey. I understand that one person in this congregation thought I was a minister who lost his congregation because of seducing church ladies. Not true."

A few in the pews dared to laugh lightly.

"The truth is that I have a doctorate but not of divinity. My doctorate is in Astronomical Engineering. I used to teach at the University of Nebraska at Lincoln. There, I also did research. I developed some processes and some instruments that have helped in both aviation and in searching the universe. I made a good deal of money from a couple of my patents. Part of that money I have put into a fund to underwrite scholarships for deserving young people such as the ones attending this church."

He looked down briefly at the Sharpe and Fowler families.

"My personal history doesn't seem appropriate for an Advent sermon. But please allow me to say more. I was raised a Lutheran. I attended church regularly. I followed the Ten Commandments. God seemed to reward me for this every step of my life. The few times I even considered my good fortune, I thought smugly that I had justified His grace. I went through university with flying colors. I landed a prestigious position. I made lots of money. I married a wonderful, beautiful, intelligent young woman. And we had two wonderful, beautiful, intelligent children."

Ernie's eyes started to cloud up. His jaw worked, and he labored to control his emotions.

"And then, one day while I was at my wonderful job, my wife was taking my children to buy clothes for school. My daughter, Elsa, was going into first grade. My son, Greg, was in pre-school. They were on the local superhighway. So was a long-haul trucker with an eighteen wheeler. He had been driving too many hours. About a thousand feet from my wife's car he fell asleep. The truck crossed the median. There was no place for my wife to go. The truck hit the car head on and destroyed it."

Ernie paused again to compose himself. "You would think there could be nothing worse than losing your wife and children instantly in a monstrous collision that was none of their causing. But there is. My son was in a car seat. The car seat protected him just enough that he was left alive. The worst of it was that he was left in a vegetative coma. Modern medicine is amazing. They can keep people alive long after..."

His voice trailed off. The sounds of sobbing echoed from every corner of the church. I, who knew the story and had had weeks to deal with it, found myself softly crying all over again.

"He lived for seven months. At first, I depended on my faith. I prayed hourly. When I was convinced there was no coming back to a normal, happy life for Gregory, I then prayed for him to die. This, too, did not happen. I stopped going to church. I stopped believing in a God who gave a damn about us. I told myself, 'If He doesn't care about us, why should I care about Him?'

"You understand I never stopped believing in God. What's the point in cursing something that doesn't exist? I merely changed my belief. I saw God as a creator who set things spinning and left. Like a novelist who writes a book. It's published. Lots of people may read it. They may desperately want the ending to change, the hero to be saved. But it doesn't change, because it is what it is.

"When Greg finally died, I couldn't bear to stay in the area. I moved out here and began work at the Institute for Advanced Studies. You know, the place in Princeton made famous by Albert Einstein. I moved into your town and purchased a large house, because I was unwilling to give up the comfortable, familiar surroundings my wife had made for me. I fled Nebraska, but I was still holding on. I was also holding onto my anger.

"The house I chose was on a road that happened to become famous for garish Christmas *season* displays. I won't say Christmas displays, because they had nothing to do with religion. They were Snoopy on his doghouse and wire reindeer, and the dad from the Simpsons in a Santa Claus suit, and elves and toys. Given my attitude toward God, you wouldn't think this would bother me. But it did. I told myself I was irritated by the stupidity of it all, the ignorance. I told myself I hated anything that even celebrated God's existence in a cockeyed way.

"And then I mocked it all publicly and was hauled into court. That's how I ended up at St. Mark's. Once here, I announced loudly that miracles never happened and that God did not care. But then I began seeing things. I wondered if I had moved to that road by chance, if I had been ordered to do community service at this church by chance, to hear the stories of other people's miracles, to watch love and faith in action all by chance.

"What I saw confused me, made me unsure and even angrier. I stirred up trouble, out to show the members of St. Mark's what hypocrites they were by never recruiting in Ashton. But that backfired on me, too. I watched tolerance, accommodation, then warmth, then affection at work. A family in this congregation suffered a double crisis this summer, and I saw the Church rally around them instantly.

"I can't say I'm totally happy about the treatment shown to Lucia Rodriguez. Perhaps it's been her own fault not telling her story either. In her case, the reason was embarrassment. We heard several weeks ago from this pulpit how no one in Jesus's time thought it a sin for an engaged woman to be pregnant. Lucia was engaged to a young man. However, when she found that she was pregnant and would soon not be able to earn the good living she had been, that young man deserted her. The priest at her church was not sympathetic to her case. I happened to her door and suggested she come to Pastor Hartmann for counseling. While she has not been welcomed without qualification, she nevertheless feels she has a spiritual home here. I took her into my home because I have more than enough room. While we have never been together as man and woman, we have grown increasingly close. We may remain together in a more permanent way. I can't say. If it is to be, it will be.

"I have been on a journey of discovery these past two years, and I'm still on it. I still wonder how Jesus could say with assurance, "Ask and it will be given you; seek and ye shall find; knock and it shall be opened to you." I still do not think every prayer is answered…at least not as we want it to be. But I have realized something else. God gave us dominion over a miraculous planet. He gave us the minds to allow men to walk on the moon, talents to write things like *Swan Lake*, and bodies magnificent enough to be able to dance to them. He gave us the means to create a world close to heaven. When we could not overcome our sins by works alone, he gave us the perfect teacher. Jesus gave us careful instruction: Love God and love each other. Take care of each other.

"Pastor Hartmann makes wonderful points with humor. I hope you'll indulge me if I try as well. You may have heard about the old man who lived in a valley. He was warned on the television and radio that a big flood was coming, but he stayed right where he was. The flood waters rose. A man in a boat came by and begged him to climb aboard. The old man said, 'I have faith in the Lord God. I have asked for His help, and He alone will save me.' The waters rose to the eaves. The old man climbed on the roof. A helicopter came by. A man with a rope begged the old man to climb up. 'No sir!' the old man yelled. "I have faith in the Lord God. I have asked for His help, and He alone will save me.' The waters rose more, and the old man drowned. Moments later, he found himself at the Pearly Gates. And he was hopping mad. 'You know, I've trusted in the Lord God all my life,' he yelled at St. Peter. 'I had faith enough to move mountains, and still God allowed me to drown.' St. Peter smirked. 'God sent you a boat and a helicopter. What more did you want?'

I believe most laughed to relieve their sadness.

"This church understands," Ernie continued. "You accept the boat and the helicopter. You love and help each other. You tolerate each other's weaknesses. You forgive.

"I have been given a healthy body. I have been given good brains. I have been led to this church and this family. I have been allowed to share my roof with one of the most charitable, Christian women who ever walked this earth. Like the prodigal son, I was dead and am alive again. These things together are indeed a miracle. And yet I dared to curse God? What more should I want?

"The answer is only two things: First, I want your forgiveness.

And second, I want very much to be a member of this church."

We at St. Mark's are Lutherans. I have always suspected the word "Lutheran" in English means "proper and formal." Lutherans do not rise from their seats in a mass, rush a pulpit, and hug the sermonizer. Well maybe once a century we will, given the right incentive.

While I watched the spontaneous outpouring of affection below me, I realized that Ernie had to deliver his sermon again at eleven o'clock. I ran home for my recorder, because I knew I had to get this right.

CHAPTER SEVENTEEN

THOSE CHURCH MEMBERS who had not volunteered for the Living Nativity kicked themselves that year. Everyone wanted to be able to say they were part of the Skytop Road Holiday Spectacular that featured a newborn baby named Joshua on the birth certificate. Although we call our savior Jesus in English and Hey-sus in Spanish, he answered to Yeshua in his time. The name means "God is salvation."

Lucia felt well enough to bring Yeshua to the manger for an hour each night. The weather was as mild as the infant. Unlike our young church women of Northern European heritage who whine to play Mary, Lucia's Latina features are much more convincing. The same was true of the baby. We found quickly that we had to place a low fence near the street to keep the curious and the overly religious from assaulting mother and child. As the line of last defense stood several shepherds and Ernie, playing Joseph.

On Christmas Eve day, Ernest Love, my dear neighbor, rigged one of the mannequins permanently over the manger, high up between his maple trees. It was not sprayed with dark foundation as the other dummies had been, to approximate accurately the skin tones of citizens of ancient Israel. It remained its original pearlescent white. It had overlarge eyes in a thin, feminine face. Her hands were long and thin, like a Parmagianino Mannerist painting. The angel had a blond, flowing wig. Her form was covered by a diaphanous robe of light blue material that fluttered with the slightest breeze, and her delicate feet protruded back at an angle. Her arms were spread in a beatific pose. Above the angel's slightly canted head shimmered a halo of golden light. She hovered on the same thin, all-but-invisible piano wire the candy-apple red sleigh had a year earlier, so that she seemed suspended in the air. Her wings were magnificent, formed of hundreds of gleaming, white feathers. Ernie had hung her so that she seemed to be looking down at the manger with a Mona Lisa smile on her face. When the real baby was not at the manger, an intense, white light shone straight upward out of it, capturing the angel in an arresting manner. Somehow, twenty feet high among the barren branches, Ernie had managed to secure a new banner. **Xmas Canceled This Year** had been replaced with **Unto Us a Son Is Given**.

Of all the elements Ernie named during his sermon concerning his miracle, nothing in my opinion can touch that of him, Lucia, and her child at the manger in front of the Love house. There, at once, were the gifts of birth and rebirth. The Biblical Joseph was a much older man than Mary. Undoubtedly the lack of mention of him during Jesus's ministry indicates his death. Although beautiful, the worries of the past months showed in Lucia's face. The Biblical Mary found herself confronted by an angel, declared the mother of God, unmarried with child, and taken to a town that was not her own to deliver him. Surely her face had born the strain. And, in spite of my husband's assertions about Jesus being born in the spring, a boy baby had arrived nearly on Christmas Eve. Perhaps Ernie is correct that God has amply gifted us but leaves us largely on our own in this life, to take care of ourselves and our neighbors. Still, I believe that every so often, if only for His own delight, He intervenes.

Perhaps the most incredible miracle of all is that the *Home News Tribune* declared "Set coordinator Hubert Jasse is a master of understatement." I must give him credit for completing his Skytop Road Holiday Spectacular creation with a brilliant star on an invisible fifty-foot pole at the turn in the end of our road. It required a cherry picker truck and six guy wires to keep it aloft, but in the cold midwinter it looks for all the heavens like the bright star described in the gospel. It is, in fact, now a permanent fixture of Skytop Road. And Hugh is more proud of that one, blessed light than all of his fireworks displays combined.

About the Author

Brent Monahan has authored more than a dozen novels. Two of his works have been made into films: one starring Peter Fonda and Oliver Reed, and the other featuring Donald Sutherland and Sissy Spacek. He has taught writing at Rutgers University, Rider University, and Westminster Choir College, even though his terminal degree was in musical arts from Indiana University, Bloomington. He lives in Yardley, Pennsylvania.

www.ingramcontent.com/pod-product-compliance
Lightning Source LLC
Chambersburg PA
CBHW071335130626
46556CB00004B/1905